DADDY'S WAITING

PEPPER NORTH

Photography by **FURIOUSFOTOG/GOLDENCZERMAK**
Cover Model **KEVIN R DAVIS**
Edited by **CHERYL'S LITERARY CORNER**

Text copyright© 2021 Pepper North
All Rights Reserved

Dr. Richards' Littles®
is a registered trademark of
With A Wink Publishing, LLC.
All rights reserved.

AUTHOR'S NOTE:

The following story is completely fictional. The characters are all over the age of 18 and as adults choose to live their lives in an age play environment.

This is a series of books that can be read in any order. You may, however, choose to read them sequentially to enjoy the characters best. Subsequent books will feature characters that appear in previous novels as well as new faces.

AN INVITATION TO BE PART OF PEPPER'S LITTLES LEAGUE!

Want to read more stories featuring Littles? Join Pepper North's newsletter. Every other issue will include a short story as well as other fun features! She promises not to overwhelm your mailbox and you can unsubscribe at any time.

As a special bonus, Pepper will send you a free collection of three short stories to get you started on all the Littles' fun activities!

Here's the link:

http://BookHip.com/FJBPQV

PART I
ESCAPING

CHAPTER 1

"Oh, no!" Marla exclaimed around the bite of salad she'd just forked into her mouth as she pushed away from the table. Her fork clattered uselessly on the floor.

"Marla?" Piper asked in concern as she jumped to her feet to try to help with whatever was happening.

Liquid splattered to the floor as Marla looked at her helplessly. "My water just broke. OMG! How embarrassing!"

"They're adults. They'll deal with it," Piper reassured her friend before grinning and adding, "The baby's coming!"

Excitement and love replaced the worry on Marla's face. She fumbled for her phone to call her husband. As she talked, Piper called for the janitor as she texted her boss that she'd take Marla to the hospital and stay with her until the baby's daddy arrived.

"Oh, no! I can't have the baby now," Marla wailed into the phone. "Mr. Braun's big presentation is tomorrow. I have so much to do."

"They'll get a replacement for you from the assistants' pool," Piper answered as the excited father tried to calm down his wife.

"No! That won't be good enough. This has to be someone sharp," Marla answered Piper. Distracted, she disconnected the call without saying goodbye to her spouse.

Marla selected another number saved on her mobile phone.

"Terry, my water just broke. Yes, it is exciting and terrifying at the same time. Listen, I don't want to leave you in a lurch for the big presentation while I'm at the hospital. No one but Piper Townie can take my place. Pull whatever strings you need to have her swapped to your office now. I'm sending her up to you."

"I'm going to take you to the hospital," Piper protested as her friend disconnected the phone.

Marla just held up one finger and selected another contact. "Hugo, can you drive me to the hospital? You're a doll! Bring towels and come to the cafeteria. My water broke."

"Done," she announced to Piper. Marla was nothing if not a powerhouse of organization. Piper had learned so much from her. "Go to my desk. I bookmarked the to-do list with a red piece of paper in my organizer. Just follow down the chart. You'll do great."

Hugo appeared with an armful of towels. Piper didn't even question where he'd gotten those in the sleek corporate office. Everyone knew Hugo for his ingenuity and insider knowledge. As the custodian arrived with his mop bucket, Hugo escorted Marla down the hall with a supportive arm around her waist as everyone shouted their "Happy Baby" wishes to her.

Piper looked at the remnants of their lunch and quickly took care of the mess. Stopping by her office to explain everything to her boss, she found one of the assistants from the pool already at her desk. Shrugging at the power of hurricane Marla, Piper reported to the CEO's office. She crossed her fingers as she sat down in her friend's chair. "Don't let me screw this up!" she thought.

"Go home, Piper. You did an amazing job today. Marla was spot on, as she always is, to recommend you to fill in. I've asked to keep you in this office during her maternity leave. I hope that will be okay with you?"

"Of course! I enjoyed today. It was challenging, but so satisfying to see the meetings go so well." Thank goodness Piper's professional side came up with appropriate words as her mind boggled at the chance to work in the highest position.

Breathing a sigh of relief, Piper stepped into the elevator when sent home. Her mind ran over the presentation and noted a few improvements. She pulled out her phone to make some notes before she forgot. A message and an adorable picture popped in from Marla's husband. The baby had arrived early in the morning and after sleeping a bit, the couple were sharing the first snapshots of their new son. She smiled at the wrinkly face.

"That must be good news," a deep voice commented from beside her as he pressed the already lit button for the lobby with his left hand.

Piper looked up into deep brown eyes. Instantly, she stood straight and lowered her phone to give him her attention. Eye-catchingly handsome, Gabriel Serrano oozed sex appeal. Dark and athletically built, he repeatedly captured her gaze. Piper had struggled not to stare at him throughout the meetings.

"Mr. Serrano," she greeted the entrepreneur whom Terry had been hoping to impress.

"Piper, right? I've never met a Piper before."

"Yes, that's me. It's not a very common name." She changed the subject back to business. "Did you enjoy your visit to our company?"

"Yes, I was very impressed. I have already set the wheels in motion for us to work together in the future. If the rest of the company is as organized as your office, it will be smooth sailing," he answered, suavely complimenting her.

As they stepped through the open elevator doors into the lobby, he asked, "I wonder if I can trouble you again. Where would be a good place for dinner? I'd like to celebrate with a delicious steak."

"A recommendation to an Argentinian for steak? Now that's really asking for me to put my neck on the line," she joked.

"You've researched Argentina. I'm impressed. Not everyone knows that we are known for raising the finest beef."

His slow smile made her heart beat faster. Piper struggled to conceal her reaction to his dark charms. That accent alone could get her.

"Let's see. The Point Grill is our most famous steakhouse in the city. It is pricey but worth it. I've been there once for a special occasion."

"Perhaps you would care to join me for dinner?" he asked smoothly, shifting closer.

"Thank you for the kind offer. I'm afraid I need to get home to my family," Piper improvised. Surely it would be unprofessional to go out with the new client.

"Then I will have to let you go this time." Gabriel eased away from her. "It has been a pleasure to meet you, Piper. I will look forward to seeing you in the future."

The devastatingly attractive man turned to walk to the front doors before looking back at Piper to add, "You will discover that I rarely do anything to be kind."

CHAPTER 2

The next morning, Piper settled at her unfamiliar desk in the CEO's office. She logged on to the computer as she checked Marla's organizer for the day's events. Getting started, she threw herself into work.

"Piper, come into my office. I like to review with Marla what worked and what we can do better after a big event like yesterday's meeting."

She grabbed that invaluable organizer and her phone, thankful for the notes she'd taken before Gabriel Serrano had wiped all thoughts from her mind. "On my way. I had a couple of suggestions."

An hour later, she emerged from the meeting with a smile. She enjoyed working with Marla's boss. "Well, my boss now for a while," she mentally corrected herself.

Piper stopped in the middle of the room at the sight of a gorgeous arrangement of vividly colored flowers. The blooms were breathtaking. Confident that the flowers to welcome Marla's baby into the world had been delivered to the office by mistake, she decided she'd take them to her friend after work.

"Wow, we impressed someone yesterday. Who sent the flowers?" Terry asked from his doorway.

"Let me check." Piper plucked the card from the plastic holder and froze when she saw her name.

"They're to me. That's weird. I don't know anyone who would send me flowers."

"There's an easy way to find out," her new boss suggested.

"Oh!" Quickly, she opened the small envelope and removed the enclosure.

Piper,
Thank you for the recommendation. I'll look forward to seeing you again.
Yours,
Gabriel

"Oh, they're from Mr. Serrano. We ran into each other in the elevator, and I suggested The Point Grill when he asked for a dinner recommendation," Piper explained.

"He must have had an excellent meal. Good call, Piper." Her boss returned to his desk to bury himself in the long line of computer messages and documents needing his attention.

Piper sat down at her desk. Unable to resist, she buried her nose in a flower. The fragrance was heavenly. Smiling, she transcribed the notes from their morning meeting into Marla's organizer so she would have the follow-up information as well. Then Piper dove into the work waiting for her.

About an hour later, her cellphone buzzed with an incoming message. Expecting it to be from Marla, impatient to know how the meeting went, Piper tapped on the screen to find:

I hope the flowers are half as enchanting as you are.

Gabriel? Piper texted back.

Have you received two flower deliveries this morning?

No, just your lovely flowers. I don't know how you got my cell number.

A shiver of foreboding traveled down her spine before she

dismissed that feeling as ridiculous. Gabriel Serrano was a powerful business executive and an insanely handsome man. He would not be interested in her for any reason other than to thank the secretary of his new colleague.

I am resourceful when I need to be. You intrigue me, Piper. Have dinner with me tonight. I will pick you up at the front door at five.

Biting her bottom lip as she read his next message, Piper hesitated, unsure what to do. There was no mistaking his intent. She was torn between excitement that the suave, powerful man was interested in her and her desire to be professional at her new job. When her phone buzzed again, she looked back at the screen.

Don't think. Five p.m. I'll look forward to seeing you.

The thrill those last simple words evoked in her shocked Piper. She'd always dreamed of a special type of lover who would be in absolute control. Squeezing her thighs together, Piper placed her phone in her desk drawer. She didn't need to decide right now. Five o'clock was hours away.

Immersed in the paperwork required to enact the agreements forged during their successful meeting, Piper pushed all thoughts from her mind as she worked. When her phone rang an hour later, she jumped and scrambled for her phone. She smiled at the screen and accepted the call.

"Hi, Marla! How are you feeling?"

"Exhausted already, but so happy!" her friend replied. "The baby is such a good boy. I'm enchanted by him."

The two chatted about the baby for several minutes before Marla revealed the real reason for her call. "So, what's up between you and Gabriel Serrano?"

"Nothing!" Piper rushed to assure her. "I'm being totally professional!"

"Really? He's absolutely yummy. I was thrilled for you when he texted asking for your cellphone number."

"I wondered where he got it. He wants to take me out to dinner. Should I go?"

"Are you nuts? Go! The contracts are already signed. He'll send his employees to the next meetings. You won't ever see him again," Marla encouraged. "Who knows? Maybe he's your one."

Piper glanced at the time—two more hours. She'd decide by then. Changing the conversation back to the baby, she asked, "What name did you decide on?"

"We were set on Christopher James, but one look at him and we knew that was the wrong name. We'll find something perfect. Maybe I should call him Gabriel."

"You!" Piper laughed. "Go be Mommy and leave me alone," she said, hanging up the phone.

What should she do? Piper brought Gabriel's message back up. After rereading their conversation, she texted back. *I'll see you at five.*

Decision made, she stowed her phone back in the drawer and threw herself back into work. Thank goodness she had a lot to do. Piper didn't have time to second or third guess herself. She looked up when Terry closed his door with a click.

"Go home, Piper. The rest of this will wait until tomorrow. Thank you for stepping in so smoothly. It's been a blessing to have you here for Marla."

"I'm enjoying being here. There's a lot of work, but it's definitely interesting," she answered with a smile. Glancing at the clock, she noticed it was almost five. Piper waved goodbye to Terry as she gathered her things quickly.

Arriving in the lobby, she looked around, not sure where she should meet Gabriel. She peeked out the front door and saw him. He stood in the middle of the busy entrance, scanning the crowd. People streamed around Gabriel as if he had a privacy bubble of space around him. As she watched, many women took obvious second looks at him. He was absolutely magnificent in his perfectly fitted suit. Eager to join him, she stepped through the door, and he spotted her immediately.

"Piper!"

Moving toward her through the crowd, he held her gaze captive. Those brown eyes seduced her with a glance. It was as if he could see into her deepest secrets. Piper felt herself responding to him instantly as desire curled inside her. When his arm wrapped around her to guide her to the waiting car, that warm hand on the small of her back seemed to burn into her flesh.

He helped her into the back seat of a luxurious sedan before sliding in next to her. "I am very glad you're joining me," he told her, leaning forward to press a soft kiss on her lips. Unable to resist his allure, Piper inhaled discreetly to savor his masculine scent as he leaned across her to pull her seatbelt over her lap. Gabriel's spicy cologne softly tantalized—not too strong that she couldn't capture the aroma of his warm skin. She squeezed her thighs together as her body responded to him further.

With a click, he secured her seatbelt. "There. All Little girls must be kept safe."

Looking at the silent driver, he instructed, "Estamos listos para salir, Pablo."

"Little girls?" she repeated, bewildered. He couldn't possibly mean...

"It's okay, Piper. Daddies recognize their Littles quickly. I'm glad to have found you."

"I don't know what to say," she confessed after trying to process his words for a few seconds.

"You have bewitched me, sweet Piper. Tell me about yourself. I want to know everything." Gabriel's deep voice held a thread of command interspersed with charm.

He turned to face her, leaning slightly forward as if capturing her every word was supremely important. Gabriel took one of her fidgeting hands to hold between his. "It's okay, Little girl. You're safe with me."

Unable to resist the mesmerizing heat of his glance, Piper nodded. She wasn't used to being the center of any man's attention. Piper dragged her thoughts away from wondering how he knew her fantasies of finding a commanding male—one who would take a Daddydom role in her life. Just like those Littles she'd read about in so many books, Piper eagerly followed his instructions and began to tell him about herself.

By the time they arrived at the restaurant, Gabriel knew almost everything about her since she had moved to the large city. He had shared a bit about his life and family in Argentina as well. She felt connected and comfortable with him. He rewarded each bit of information with enticing smiles and warm caresses to her cheek, arm, or knee.

Inside the exclusive restaurant, he ignored the admiring glances of gorgeous women that followed them to their table. Piper loved being envied by them. She'd never been the woman everyone wanted to switch places with.

When he ordered seafood for her, Piper didn't interrupt. She could eat around her allergy. She was sure she'd be okay. Carefully avoiding the shrimp floating in the delicious sauce, Piper felt the first tingling spot on her right cheek.

No! Please! She dug her fingers into the palm of her left hand as she struggled not to scratch. Piper tried to keep her face angled away from him so he wouldn't see the welt on her face.

"Piper? What is wrong?" Gabriel cupped her chin and turned it toward him.

When her gaze dropped to her plate automatically, he guessed, "You're allergic to seafood? Why didn't you tell me?" Gabriel raised a hand to signal the waiter. His immediate arrival prevented her from answering.

"Our bill, please."

"I hope nothing is wrong with your meal," the skilled server attempted to assist.

"No, something urgent has come up." Gabriel handed the man his credit card to speed up the process.

"Right away, sir."

"I didn't want to interrupt our meal. It's just a silly allergy. Nothing important. I'll take some pills when I get home and all the spots will disappear soon," she promised as he tapped something into his phone.

"There is no such thing as a silly allergy. Reacting to seafood can be deadly."

The server's arrival saved her from needing to answer. Surreptitiously, she scratched at a welt just under the hem of her dress. The spots were beginning to drive her crazy. Cursing herself for being so stupid, Piper knew she'd never see Gabriel again.

"Let's go, Piper." He swept her out of the restaurant smoothly. The car met them at the entrance. Gabriel fastened her inside and captured both hands so she couldn't scratch.

"Do you need to go to the hospital?" he asked, holding her gaze.

"No. Really, I'll be okay. I just need to take some medicine at home."

"What's your address?" he requested, smiling as she recited her address. "Pablo." The car pulled smoothly into traffic and headed to her apartment.

He spoke to her calmly, describing the beauty of his home. The pictures he drew in her mind helped distract her from the itching. She listened, adding Argentina to her bucket list of places she wished to visit sometime.

Thank goodness the traffic was light, allowing them to cross from the affluent section to the lower middle-class area where she lived. When they arrived at her building, Gabriel swept her inside and stepped into the elevator with her. Piper didn't think about the dangers of inviting a relatively unknown man into her home until they stood at her door.

"Thank you for bringing me home. I'll be fine now," she rushed to assure him.

"I'm not leaving until I'm sure you're okay, Piper," he answered, taking her keys and opening the door.

Gabriel ushered her inside. "Go get your medicine and take off this fitted dress for something more flowing," he directed.

Piper fled for the bathroom and fumbled through the drawer to find her allergy medicine. Downing two tablets with a gulp of water, she grabbed a tube of anti-itch medicine and smoothed the cooling gel over the welt on her face. She exhaled in relief before all the other spots rebelled, demanding her attention.

Walking into her closet, she ripped the form-fitting dress from her body and coated every spot she could reach. There were several on her back that eluded her touch. As she waited for the gel to dry, she debated her choices of things to wear. Nothing would be attractive. Her fuzzy robe would be soft but hot. Piper rejected that idea. Her gaze landed on the enveloping cotton swimsuit coverup that hung at the rear of the rack of clothes. Grabbing that, she pulled it over her head.

She paused before rounding the corner into the sitting area. Piper certainly didn't want him to see her like this. Looking down, she stepped slightly into view.

"Gabriel, I'm fine now. Thank you for bringing me home for the medicine. I'm sorry I worried you."

"Come here, Piper." Gabriel stretched out a hand for hers.

Unable to resist, she walked toward him. His eyes scanned her body, noting the red patches that dotted her skin. When she reached him, his gaze was hard.

"I'm sorry," she whispered, coming to a stop before him.

"You put yourself in harm's way when a simple comment could have avoided all this discomfort."

"It's getting better already," she insisted. The combination of the gel and the tablets had soothed the worst of the itch.

He looked at her carefully, assessing the welt on her cheek. "It does appear to be easing. That is good. I would not wish to punish you while you are at risk."

"Punish me?" she laughed, her voice sounding high-pitched.

"Little girls who endanger themselves need a reminder to act better in the future." Gabriel tugged her after him as he walked slowly to the couch. He seated himself on the edge of the cushions and pulled her to stand next to him. "Lie over my lap, Piper."

She stared at him, unable to believe what he was asking her. Instant heat pooled in her lower abdomen. Surely this wasn't happening. He didn't plan to... "You aren't going to spank me. I mean—people don't really do that, do they?"

"Daddies of misbehaving Littles do. Over my lap." Gabriel tugged her, sending her off balance. "This way. I am left-handed." He easily moved her into the correct position before she could react and struggle. Pulling her loose cover up, he draped it over her shoulders to expose her back.

"Oh, Little one. Look what you have done to yourself." His fingertip traced the edge of one of the large red patches on her back.

She shivered as it flamed into itching. He'd found the ones she hadn't been able to reach. "I have some topical medicine…"

"I will treat it after." His fingers hooked in the back of her panties and pulled them down to mid-thigh.

"No!" she protested, wiggling on his lap as Piper finally realized that he was serious.

Whack! Whack! His hand landed hard on her bottom. Piper reared up, her torso arching away from the floor. Gabriel continued to pepper her rounded flesh with sharp smacks. She lurched one way and then the other, trying to break the hold he had on her, but nothing worked.

The heat built in her skin under his punishment. Each spank wasn't overwhelming by itself, but the combination of the spanks wiped all thoughts from her mind. Piper collapsed over his legs, unable to hold her body up any longer. She covered her face with her hands as tears welled from her eyes and spilled down to soak into the gray carpet below her.

"Gabriel, no. Please stop. I'm sorry. I'll never bother you again. You can just go," she offered.

"Ah, no, Little one. You have provoked the Daddy inside me. I won't disappear from your life now. I'm here to take care of you. Count the last five swats with me, Piper, to complete your punishment."

"Please!" she begged, before choking out, "One."

When she announced, "Five," Gabriel tenderly lifted her up to lie against his chest. He whisked her panties from around her ankles, where they had tumbled. Pulling his handkerchief from his pocket, he slipped the scrap of lace in its place. Gabriel wiped the mess her nose had created during her sobs without a comment before pressing a soft kiss to her lips. Gathering her to him, his hands soothed over her back and arms as she melted against him.

"Shh, Little one. You are fine. Daddy will protect you from now on," he soothed as he rubbed her back.

"Daddy?" The question tumbled from her lips.

"Yes, every Little girl needs her Daddy. You just hadn't found yours yet."

"You're going to be my Daddy?" she whispered.

"Forever and ever."

CHAPTER 3

What seemed like hours later, Piper felt herself gel back together. It was the strangest feeling, as if Gabriel had reduced her to her most basic form and then comforted her as she settled into that quiet space. She felt closer to him than any boyfriend she'd ever cared about. The thought registered that Gabriel was not a boy, making her laugh.

"Oh, to know the thoughts going on in your brain, Little girl," Gabriel chuckled. "You are feeling better, aren't you?"

"Yes... Daddy?" She hesitated before trying out the new name.

"Very good, Piper. That deserves a reward. Come, let Daddy put you to bed." He stood, lifting her effortlessly in his arms.

Gabriel walked to her bedroom and placed Piper on her feet. Moving her teddy bear over to the side, he threw back the covers before turning back to her. After kissing her forehead lightly, he unzipped her coverup. Automatically, Piper held the edges together. "No, Little girl. No hiding from your Daddy. I will see all of you."

Forcing her fingers to release the fabric, he pushed it off her shoulders and let it tumble to the floor. Gabriel smoothed a fingertip over the lacy edge of one bra cup, making her shiver in reaction to the light touch on her sensitive breast. "Very pretty, but a big girl wears this."

His finger lingered at the hollow between her breasts, as if to capture her attention, before tracing over the front closure. With a flick of that finger, he unfastened it. Automatically, she moved to shield her breasts but froze at his tsk, tsk, tsk. Piper forced her hands back to her sides.

"Good girl."

The praise shouldn't have made her happy, but it thrilled her to have pleased him. Piper stood still as Gabriel smoothed the straps one by one off her shoulders and dropped the garment to the floor. She froze as he stepped back to scan her body.

What if he didn't like what he saw? Her every imperfection haunted her thoughts as she dropped her gaze to his shiny leather wingtips.

"Turn around slowly, Little girl," he commanded.

Unable to stop herself, Piper obeyed. She rotated bit by bit, jumping when he reached out to squeeze one of her punished cheeks.

"Your bottom looks enchanting wearing the proof of your submission," Gabriel complimented.

With a light tap on her sore skin, he directed, "Continue, Piper."

When she faced him once again, Gabriel stepped forward. His hand smoothed over her back to cup the same buttock, pulling her tightly against his body. Breath rushed into her lungs at the feel of his thick erection. A feeling of elation filled her as she realized she had aroused him.

"You please me, Little girl. Now, it's time for a bedtime story before I tuck you in bed. Sit on the edge of your mattress."

He waited for her to comply before giving the next instruction. "Lie back and spread your legs wide."

"What?" she asked, doubting that she had heard him correctly.

"Your red bottom doesn't wish to be spanked again tonight, Piper. Lie back and spread your legs." He waited as she slowly followed his instructions.

"Wider."

Feeling her face heat with embarrassment, Piper spread her legs as wide as possible. She watched him scan her body from her red face to the intimate display between her legs. Gabriel shifted his erection inside his fine wool slacks before athletically dropping to his knees.

"Good Little girls deserve rewards." Gabriel captured her gaze before lowering his mouth.

The intimacy of watching him as he inhaled an inch from her body pushed Piper's arousal higher than it ever had been. When he lapped at the juices coating her intimate folds, his "mmm" of pleasure reverberated through her. Finally, he gave her permission to just feel.

"Close your eyes, Little girl."

Gabriel demanded her response. Using his tongue and fingers, he quickly drove her into an orgasm that shook her body with its intensity. Her fingers curled into the covers as she held on for stability in the whirling sensations he evoked. As soon as one climax faded, he altered his approach to push her into the next.

When she begged for him to stop, he chuckled against her. "One more, Little girl."

Lifting her boneless form into his arms, Gabriel shifted her to rest against the pillows. She felt his kiss and smiled tiredly against his lips.

"Tell Daddy thank you for taking care of you," he directed.

"Thank you, Daddy," she parroted.

"Of course, Little girl."

Gabriel collected the gel she'd left out on the counter in the bathroom and carefully smoothed it over the last remaining welts on her skin. "Go to sleep, Piper. Here's your stuffie," he said as he tucked the well-loved bear into her arms.

"Dream of Daddy," he whispered as he smoothed the covers into place.

She nodded as she dropped into sleep.

CHAPTER 4

Gabriel wooed her as if she were a princess in a fairytale, showering her with flowers and romantic outings. Piper loved walking out of the building each night to find him waiting. She never knew what he had planned, only that she would love every moment.

Forcing herself to focus on business during the day, Piper enjoyed her new responsibilities and duties as the administrative assistant to the CEO. Her efforts were not overlooked, and her boss relied on her more and more as Marla's maternity leave continued.

One Friday, a messenger delivered a new dress to Piper's office. She caressed the soft fabric, desperate to try it on. Glancing at Terry's closed door, she decided to take her boss up on his offer to let her work from home that afternoon while he was gone. Gathering a stack of paperwork she would force herself to complete after seeing if the dress fit, Piper caught the bus back to her apartment.

Moments later, twirling in front of the mirror, Piper pressed Gabriel's number. "It's beautiful."

"I never anticipated anything else. Wear it tonight. I'll pick you up at five?"

"That's wonderful. Make it six if that's okay. I want to primp at home a bit to look worthy of this dress."

"You'll outshine the fabric easily, Little girl. Shall I come to your apartment?" he asked.

"Yes, please. I'm home now. I brought a few things with me from the office to work on, and then I'll plunge into beauty treatments," she promised.

"I'll look forward to seeing you soon."

"Piper, you look ravishing, my sweet." Gabriel tucked a large envelope under one arm as he took her hands and stepped back to study her. The heat filling his eyes when he met her gaze kindled the desire low in her stomach.

"Thank you for the dress, Gabriel. It is exquisite."

"Daddies love to spoil their Little girls, Piper. It's what we do," he shared with a big smile.

She could tell he was very pleased. Feeling her face heat under his perusal, Piper tried to shift the conversation. "What's in the envelope, Daddy?"

"Something important for us to discuss later." Releasing one of her hands, Gabriel placed the envelope on her table where her completed paperwork sat neatly stacked.

Pointing to the computer as if it jogged his memory, he added, "I started to send you a message this afternoon and realized I didn't have your email address. Turn on your computer and type in mine so I'll have yours to reply to."

"We can do that later, Daddy," she suggested, picking up her purse to leave.

"Now, Piper," Gabriel corrected with steel in his voice. "We will forget later."

She sat down at the table and typed in her four-number security code when the machine woke up. Piper hated to wait for it to power on, so she simply sent it to sleep when she wasn't using it. Quickly, she sent him a message to the email address he dictated before again sending the computer into waiting mode.

"Thank you, Piper. Now I will not have to think about it later. Let's go to dinner. I'm looking forward to showing you off." Smiling once again, he ushered her out of the apartment and down to the waiting car.

"Do you ever drive yourself?" she wondered as they merged into traffic.

"Only dangerously fast cars I would not risk you riding in," he answered smoothly. "I would much prefer to do this," Gabriel leaned in to kiss her soundly, "than concentrate on driving."

Pleased with his attention, Piper leaned close. "Where are we headed to for dinner, Gabriel?"

At his pointed look of disapproval, she whispered, "Daddy?" Piper peeked forward to where the driver sat, uncomfortable with others knowing her secret.

"Pablo is only an employee, Piper. He would not dare to gossip about his employer, or he would soon be out of a job."

Piper's tender heart went out to the man, skillfully negotiating through the traffic. She knew he followed the entire conversation despite his impassive expression. Pablo had to realize that no matter how well he did his job, he would always be an easily replaceable employee. She glanced back at Gabriel's face, hoping to see a bit of compassion.

"You are not used to my world, Piper. Leave it to me to take care of all the necessities of life. Let's enjoy our evening together," Gabriel urged, perhaps sensing her discomfort. "Tonight, we are going to a beautiful restaurant. It is time I celebrated my beautiful Little girl. Everyone will be envious of me tonight."

"I like the sound of us celebrating." Piper allowed herself to be distracted from the negative thoughts.

When they pulled up in front of the most exclusive restaurant in town, Piper turned to look at Gabriel in astonishment. "We're eating here? It's so expensive, Gabriel. We could celebrate somewhere else."

"Here is where we will dine, Piper. Allow Pablo to open your door," he ordered as he slid from the car. Rounding the trunk, he extended his hand to take hers, assisting her from the sedan.

Piper clung to his arm as they crossed the beautiful waiting area.

Immediately, the maître d' greeted Gabriel, "Sr. Serrano. It is a pleasure to have you join us for dinner. I have placed your champagne on ice at your table. Please follow me."

"Champagne?" Piper whispered.

Gabriel didn't answer her question, but led her to the secluded table where a large silver bucket stood, holding a wrapped bottle inside. The hovering waiter carefully placed the napkin on Piper's lap after Gabriel seated her.

"Good evening, sir, miss. I am William. I will take care of you tonight."

"Good evening, William. I hope you received my orders," Gabriel asked.

"Yes, sir." The server lifted the bottle from the ice and displayed it for his approval.

"Perfect. Please open the bottle for us," Gabriel instructed. When they each held a glass of the effervescent liquid, he focused on Piper.

"To us, Piper," he proposed, clinking his glass lightly against hers.

Obediently, Piper took a sip before peering over the glass at him. "Is there an us?" she asked bravely.

"Very definitely," he answered with a captivating smile.

Taking another sip, Piper studied him over the rim. She didn't understand why Gabriel, with his model-like good looks and slim, hard body, would be interested in her. Only an idiot would miss the flirtatious looks and open invitations many of the women in the restaurant offered him. Distracted by her thoughts, she missed seeing him reach into his pocket to withdraw a small velvet box.

The sparkle of finely cut diamonds caught her attention. Piper heard, "Look, he's proposing," drift from another table.

Shocked, she met his dark eyes. Her heart raced in her chest. *Surely not...*

"Little girl, you have forever enchanted me. Will you grant me my deepest wish and become Mrs. Gabriel Serrano?"

"Gabriel?" she whispered, sure she must be imagining this.

"Say yes, Piper," he urged with an indulgent smile.

"Yes!" burst from her lips in a whisper of a sound, as if she were afraid to speak loudly enough to wake herself from this dream.

After plucking the exquisite engagement ring from the box, Gabriel took her left hand. He lifted it first to his lips and then slid the ring onto her third finger. As delighted applause rang out around the exclusive dining room, Gabriel claimed her, "My Little girl forever."

The rest of the meal was a blur. Piper knew she ate some of the food placed in front of her as the champagne flowed. Finally, they shared a rich chocolate dessert. As Gabriel placed a bite in her mouth, he shared, "Tonight, I will make you mine completely. Are you ready to leave, Piper?"

Swallowing quickly, she nodded. "Please, Gabriel. Take me home."

Efficiently, he settled the bill and accepted the congratulations of several people as they walked through the tables of elegantly dressed patrons. During the ride home, Gabriel tantalized her with passionate kisses and intimate touches. The champagne clouded her awareness, so she didn't even think of Pablo until he opened the door for her.

"Thank you, Pablo," she whispered, not meeting his eyes.

"May you be very happy, miss," he congratulated her.

Gabriel whisked her away into her apartment. His hands skillfully stripped Piper's clothing from her. "Such a beautiful Little girl," he praised, tracing her curves with his fingers.

She gasped and clung to his broad shoulders as Gabriel lifted her into his arms. His mouth captured hers in a hard kiss that revealed his desire. Striding through her apartment by memory, he carried her into her bedroom, as he had every evening since they met. This time, she knew he wouldn't just tuck her in bed after bringing her pleasure.

Placed in the center of the bed, Piper watched as he disrobed. Dark hair scattered over his chiseled chest. A thin line trailed into his fine trousers. She held her breath as he unfastened his pants, pushing them carelessly over his hips to puddle below her view. His shaft pressed fiercely against the black knit boxers that hugged his body. When those, too, dropped to the floor, Piper lurched up from her back to reach for him. His low chuckle at her eagerness made her freeze in place.

"Patience, Little girl." Gabriel crawled onto the bed and moved to cage her under his body. He captured her mouth and took control of the kiss, pressing his tongue inside to taste her. "Mmm."

"Please, Gabriel! Touch me." Piper swept her hands down his sides, enjoying the strength in his muscular body. Daringly, she brushed down his spine to cup his buttocks. Her world twirled around her as Gabriel rolled them over to drape her on top of him. She sat up partially in shock at the sudden move and froze when his shaft pressed intimately against her.

Gabriel cupped her breasts as he curled his torso up to press another kiss to her lips. Lowering himself to rest against the pillows, his eyes feasted on her body as she gyrated against his cock. Her plentiful juices allowed her to slide over his erection. His fingers closed on her nipples, treating them to a taste of pain before he soothed them with a swirl of his tongue.

When the fingers of one hand traced a fiery path to her pussy, Piper lifted herself slightly to give him access. As her reward, Gabriel traced her clit with one fingertip. Trapped between wanting to press against him and fear that he would stop, Piper held her breath, holding for the pleasure that Gabriel lavished on her so easily.

As he stroked her, Gabriel asked, "Are you ready to join with me, Little one? I will never let you go after this."

"Please, Gabriel. I need you so badly."

"In my jacket pocket is a silver card case. Get it for me."

"What?" she asked in confusion.

"Get it for me, Little girl."

Scrambling, she moved off him and slid from the bed. Remembering that he had hung his jacket from the chair in her room, Piper searched in one pocket and then the other. She turned triumphantly with the heavy case in her hand. Climbing back on the bed, Piper delivered it to him.

"Daddies need to protect their Little girls," Gabriel announced, pulling the top off to reveal a strip of condoms.

She watched, mesmerized by the sight of his hands moving on his cock. Without being asked, Piper moved back into position, straddling his pelvis. Encircling her waist with his hands, Gabriel urged her higher and pressed himself against her opening.

Piper's breath caught in her throat as he entered her. His thickness stretched her wide as he slowly helped lower her body over his shaft.

Finally, she rested fully against his pelvis. She panted in reaction as he seemed to fill every fraction of an inch inside her.

When his thumb stroked roughly across her clit, Piper rocked against his body. Tingles of pleasure gathered inside her. Just out of reach, she chased the pleasure as he moved. Higher and higher, he built the wave threatening to crash over her until she couldn't handle any more.

"Please, Daddy. Help me!" Piper begged. She clung to him as once again, he rolled them over.

"Yes!" she encouraged as his thrusts into her strengthened. Piper's fingers bit into his shoulders, and she strained toward her climax.

"Come now, Piper!" he commanded.

Seconds later, the sensations peaked. With a cry, she exploded around him.

Gabriel tucked the covers around her chin before pressing a kiss to her forehead. "Sleep, Little girl. Soon, you will be mine forever."

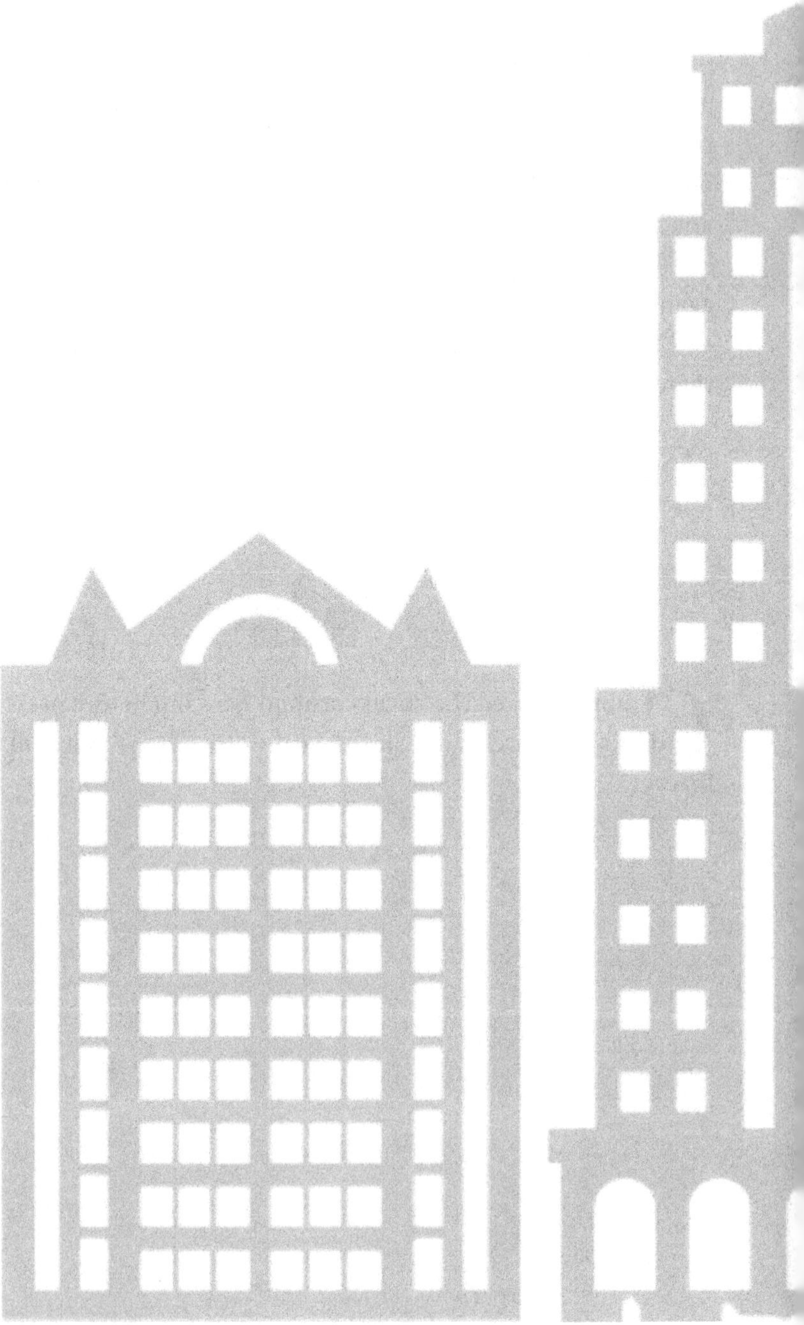

CHAPTER 5

"Piper, I feel you are being wasted in your former position. Your boss has asked when I'm sending you back and I'll admit, I don't want to. Have you talked to Marla?" Terry asked.

"Not this week," Piper admitted, feeling like a rotten friend. She'd been so busy with Gabriel that she hadn't texted back when she'd received the last batch of cute baby pictures.

"She notified me today that she is going to stay home with the baby for a while and will not be returning when her maternity leave ends. I'd like to offer you her position."

"Really? I'd love to keep working with you." Piper tried to react professionally, but inside she jumped up and down in excitement.

"Now, you have to promise you won't let Gabriel Serrano charm you away from me. I understand he is opening an office here," Terry commented.

She sensed he was half kidding, half serious. "My personal life and professional life won't ever overlap. That's a recipe for disaster," Piper assured him.

"Sometimes, hearts and brains don't check with each other, but I'm glad to have your help," Terry wisely answered.

"Thank you for taking a chance on me, Terry. I'll work hard," she promised.

"Why didn't you tell me you were opening an office here?" Piper asked that evening when Gabriel picked her up.

"Watch your tone, Little girl. Daddies don't have to tell their Little girls everything. Perhaps I wanted it to be a surprise."

Immediately, Piper apologized, "Oh, I'm sorry, Daddy."

"Apology accepted."

When she thought back to the conversation the next morning, Piper realized he hadn't ever answered her. He'd only suggested that perhaps it was a surprise. Maybe it wasn't.

Shaking her head at this negative thought, Piper chided herself, sure that she was reading into his lack of words. Gabriel satisfied her most secret desires—those she'd never planned to share with anyone. He just knew what she needed.

To distract herself, she sent a quick message to Marla with her congratulations that the new mom could stay home with her baby. Immediately, her phone buzzed. Expecting a tickled response, Piper's mouth dropped open as she read: *I can't believe you repaid my trust and friendship by filling Terry's head with all that garbage. Karma is usually a bitch, and I can't wait until she catches up with you!*

To her further astonishment, she found Marla had blocked her number when she quickly texted back, *What are you talking about?*

When Terry walked through the room, she asked, "Marla just sent me a baffling message."

"I can't imagine that she's too pleased with you for revealing her incompetence," Terry answered wryly.

"What? I've never said anything bad about Marla! She's an amazing administrative assistant. She taught me so much," Piper protested.

"Really? That report definitely didn't pull any punches."

"What report?" she asked, mind boggled.

"Let me pull it up on my computer," Terry said, obviously sensing something was amiss.

Piper followed him into the office and watched as he opened a file to select a Word document. He turned the computer around so that she could see a file of events. After reading the first couple, she looked at him in shock. "That never happened."

"Then why did you send it?" he asked, steepling his fingers together as he looked sternly at her.

"I didn't. I've never seen that before."

"It came after hours from your personal account," Terry reported, turning the computer back to face him. He pulled up an email and turned it to show her.

"Terry, I didn't send that. I don't know who hacked my account and sent that, but it wasn't me. Marla is… was my friend and mentor. She's amazing. How can I fix this?"

He shook his head sadly. "I don't know. I forwarded it to HR and they offered her the chance to resign before being dismissed."

"Let's figure this out." He selected a number from his address book. Marla's hesitant "hello" sounded in the room.

"Thank you for taking my call, Marla. Something's going on here that I don't like, and I want to get to the bottom of it. I want you to know that Piper is here with me."

"I don't wish to talk to her," Marla snapped.

"I think we need her here. You should know that without her concern that something awful had happened, we would not be talking this afternoon. I was convinced by the information that had arrived by email from Piper's personal address. She states she has never seen this before. Unless she is a polished actress, my gut says she's telling the truth," Terry attested.

"Marla, I don't know where that came from. I didn't make that list," Piper protested.

"Then where did it come from?" Marla challenged.

"The email date is on Friday, a week ago. Terry was out of the office in meetings all day long. I took some work home with his permission and worked there. I wanted some extra time to get ready for my date with Gabriel. He asked me to marry him at dinner. I always leave my computer on standby. Maybe someone hacked into it?" Piper spoke slowly as she tried to remember all the events of that evening. Her face heated, remembering how passionately Gabriel had made love to her that first time.

"The easier answer would be that Gabriel sent it," Marla jabbed.

Piper's mouth dried in an instant. Her mind recreated the slant of the laptop as if someone left-handed had used it. He wouldn't have, would he?

"Terry, Gabriel mentioned a new agreement that he was brokering between the two companies. Have you made any decision about it?" Piper asked, rapidly changing the subject.

"There are no new agreements," Terry refuted. "Let's get back to the statement that was sent to me..." His voice faded out as Piper dashed into the adjoining office to rifle through the papers on her desk.

"What's going on?" Marla's voice demanded.

"I don't know. Piper has run into her office to grab something. Here, she's back." Terry accepted a sheet of paper from his new admin's trembling hand. "What? An agreement for our company to order exclusively from the Serrano Corporation. I would never agree to this. Where did this come from?"

"It was in a stack of papers you placed in my inbox," Piper explained. "I didn't process it because it seemed off somehow."

"Was this in the papers you took home to work on last week?" Terry asked.

Piper swallowed hard and nodded. They were the papers she had left out on her desk that evening when Gabriel had asked her to marry him. She twisted the ornate engagement ring on her finger. "I don't understand what's going on, but I know Marla is innocent of all those charges. I'll tender my resignation so she can come back to work."

Terry and Marla spoke at the same time. He broke off to listen to her response.

"I was horribly hurt when I was accused of such an awful list of policy violations. I no longer wish to return to that position. I would like to have all my severance pay with a bonus for the treatment I received. I would also like to have a document stating that the allegations are incorrect and that this company will provide a spotless reference when I return to work," Marla demanded immediately.

Piper nodded at her friend's fast-thinking mind. Marla would land on her feet. Her anxiety over hurting her friend eased a bit. Staying at home with the baby had always been Marla's dream. Piper bet Terry would make sure her severance package was generous.

Terry disconnected the call. "Piper," he said gently to draw her away from her tumultuous thoughts, "I do not wish to accept your resignation, but I feel I must if you don't realize what connects all these events. There is only one person who would have benefited if you'd completed that paperwork."

"Gabriel," she breathed heavily, feeling sick.

"I'd like you to take the rest of the day off. Come back Monday morning and we'll discuss what we need to do next."

Nodding, she turned to walk to the door. Piper looked over her shoulder to apologize. "I feel like such a fool. I'm so sorry for not seeing what was going on."

"We'll talk Monday, Piper."

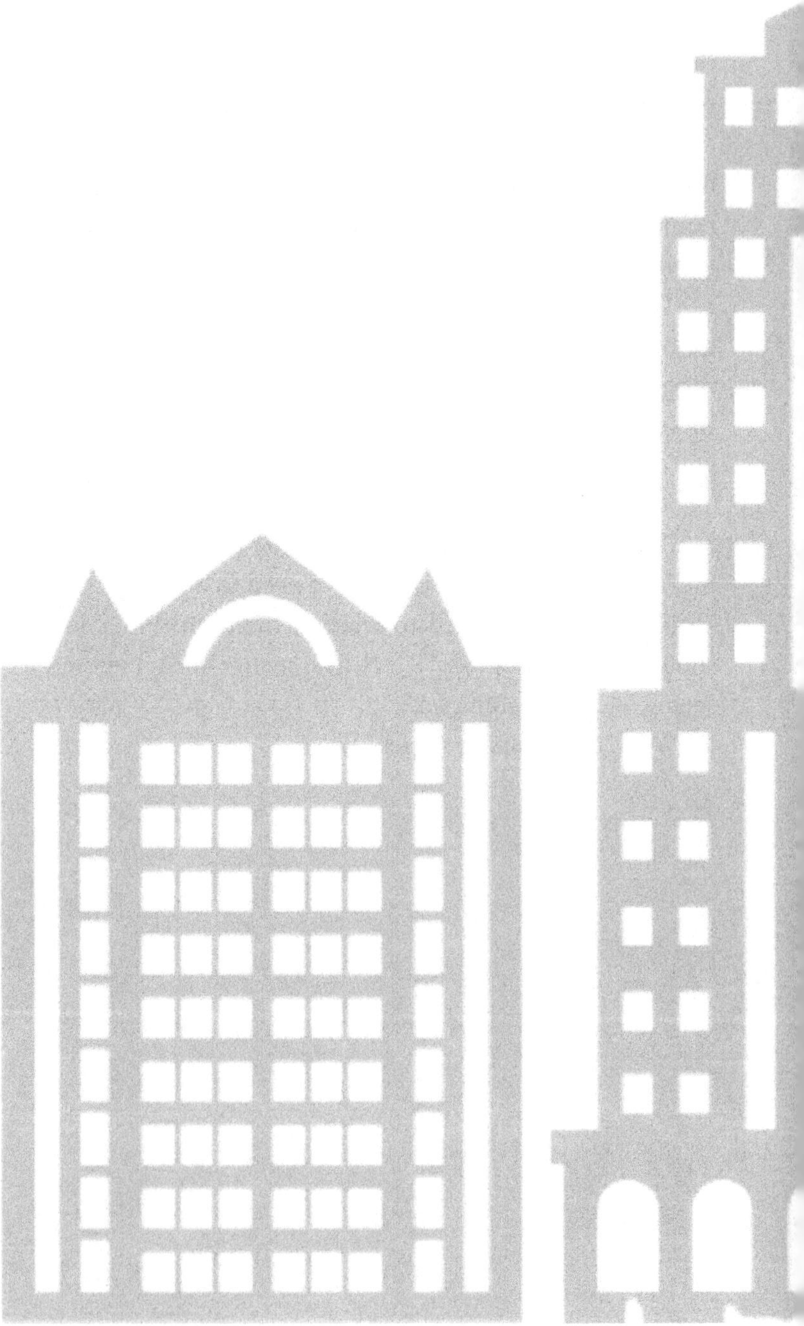

CHAPTER 6

Walking out of the office, Piper realized she didn't even know where to go to confront Gabriel. She pulled out her phone and messaged him. *Where are you?*

You are eager to see me, Little fiancée? I am at my hotel. I am getting tired of living here at the Continental. Perhaps we should look for a house this weekend.

She began walking. The Continental was three blocks east from her office. Piper ignored it when she felt her phone buzz insistently. Walking through the immense glass doors, she texted, *I'm here. Please come to the lobby.*

I dislike your tone, Little girl. Come to room 523.

She knew better than to meet with him alone. Walking to the concierge, Piper asked to leave a message with him for a guest. When he provided her with an envelope, she tugged off her ring and dropped it inside.

"That is too valuable to leave with me. Allow me to call," he glanced at the name she'd scrawled on the envelope for room five twenty-three, "Mr. Serrano."

"I really don't care whether or not the ring disappears." Piper turned and left.

Once at home, she looked around, seeing Gabriel's presence stamped on her apartment. She packed a garment bag with several work outfits and loaded her most precious possessions into a large duffle bag. A polite knock sounded at her door, making her freeze. Quietly, she crept to the door and looked through the viewfinder. Pablo.

"I'm not going with you, Pablo."

"I will inform Sr. Serrano," he promised.

When she watched him continue to stand at the door, she flung it open. "Go away, Pablo."

He looked past her to the quickly packed bags. "Run far away and do not let him find you, Piper."

Her anger deflated as she realized he wouldn't force her to go with him. "That's my plan."

"I will call him in two minutes to tell Sr. Serrano that you were not here. He will not take my word for it."

"I'll go now."

Pablo nodded. "Do not let him find you," he repeated before turning and walking to the elevator.

Loading her arms, Piper raced down the stairway to the parking garage. She would stay with her parents for a few days to let him calm down.

Driving down the gravel path, Piper relaxed for the first time. Gabriel had never asked about her family in their whirlwind courtship. He definitely didn't know where they lived. The trail of dust alerted her parents that someone approached. By the time she parked in front of their house, they waited on the porch.

"Piper, honey. We didn't know you were coming," her mother greeted her with a wide smile.

"Mom!" Her voice trembled with the stress and emotions she'd bottled up during the drive. "I have so much to tell you."

Listening to her own story, Piper wondered if everything had actually happened. It seemed so unreal. Her phone remained silent. Gabriel appeared to have given up. Accompanying her parents to church on Sunday morning, Piper felt safe in her small community.

On the way home, her dad spotted a plume of dissipating dust coming from the farm. Pointing it out, he asked, "Do you think your young man would come to find you?"

"I don't think he's that stupid. We would call the police immediately," her mother soothed when Piper stiffened. "I'm sure a neighbor just dropped off a jar of beets or something special for Piper."

"No, he's very smart."

Parking in the garage, her father searched the house before allowing the women inside. "No one's here. We're all on edge, I think."

Walking into her room, Piper discovered that her father had missed something. Her childhood stuffed bear, Stanley, wasn't in the center of her bed as normal. His head lay on the pillow with the covers perfectly arranged around him. Gabriel's precision in tucking her in at night flashed into her mind. In two steps, she reached the bed and flung the covers back. A scrap of red lace rested below the stuffie.

Unable to stop herself, she picked them up. Rocking back on her heels, Piper flashed back to that night after her spanking. He had taken her panties. Swallowing hard, she knew he'd been there, and she needed to leave.

She couldn't go back to her apartment. The city where Gabriel had settled would be the worst place to be. Contacting Terry, she confessed almost the whole story, leaving out the intimate parts he didn't need to know. "I'm sorry, Terry. I'm not safe there. In a few minutes, I'll send you my resignation. I'm sorry to leave you in a lurch."

"And I feel responsible for doing business with him. Thank goodness you realized that something was off with that agreement. I can cut ties with him in three months now. When you find another job, use my name as a reference. Your skills as an administrative assistant have been remarkable."

"Thank you, Terry."

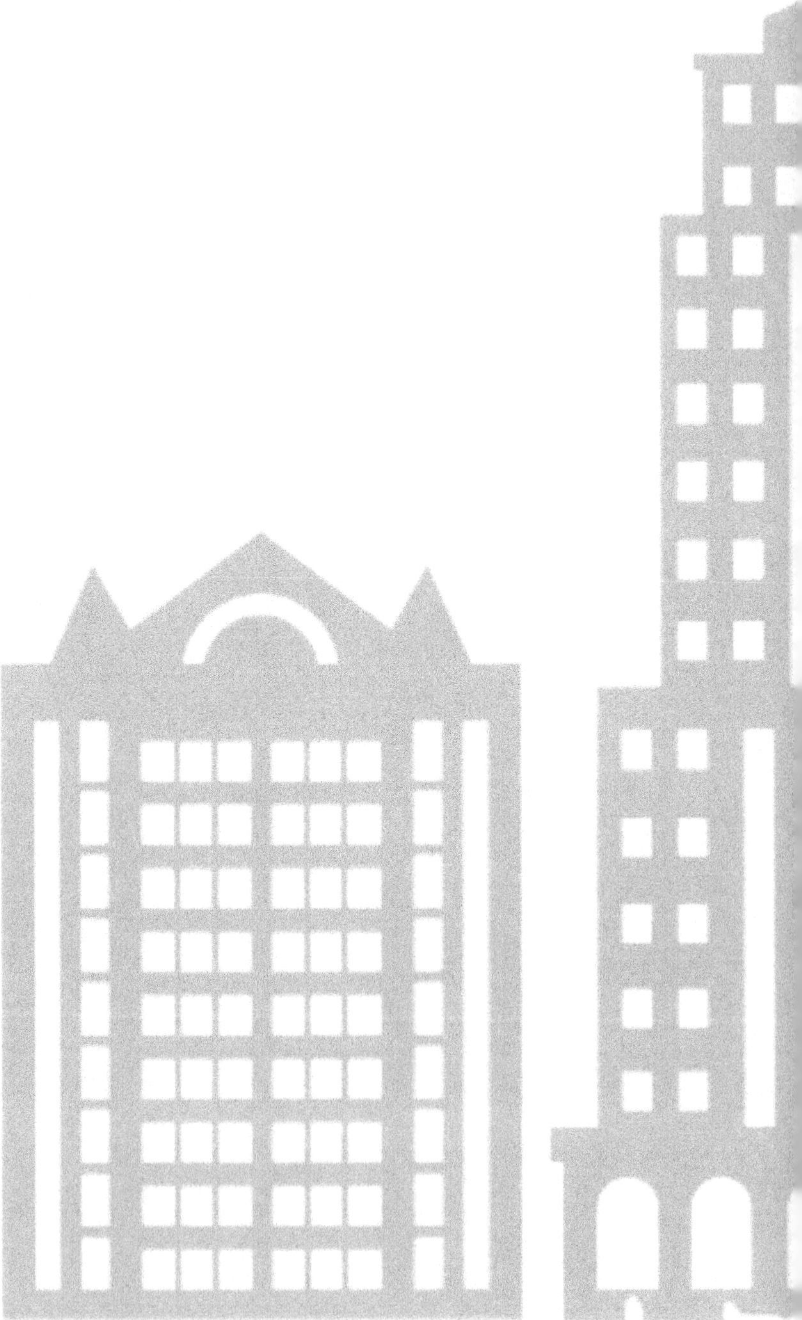

CHAPTER 7

"Good morning, Mr. Edgewater!" one of the weekend security guards greeted.

"Morning, Jason! How's your bride?" Easton Edgewater asked through the window of his SUV.

"She's settling into her new life well, sir. Thank you for asking." The recently married young man beamed.

Easton waved as he drove on through the manned gate securing the ABC Towers. Jason and his bride, Tori, had invited the entire staff to the small service held in the rose garden of the complex. Easton's attendance had created a buzz from their families, who didn't understand what a close relationship most employees had in his corporation.

This morning, he looked around in approval as he drove into the company he had established through hard work, brilliant strategy, and yes, a lot of luck. The grounds of the building complex were immaculate. Experts had designed them to provide outdoor spaces for any activities his employees needed: a walking trail, lunch in the fresh air, festivities. Easton had gathered the latest in innovative wellness and happiness concepts to create a mecca for everyone who worked there. To his delight, a thriving community of his employees now surrounded the three towers on two sides. He also owned the unsettled area on the other two sides for miles to ensure for future expansion.

Parking in his reserved spot by the private elevator of the A building, Easton grabbed his computer case and overnight case from the rear. He used a key fob to trigger the door to open as he approached. Accessing the elevator, he pressed the top button to his office and private quarters.

"Good morning, Easton," his administrative assistant called from her desk. "I'm glad you're home. Coffee?"

"I'd love it, Sharon. Thank you. You didn't need to come in today," he added, smiling at her dedication.

"I left a file on your desk. I'll admit, I'm eager to hear your reaction," Sharon confessed.

Intrigued by the hint of nervousness in his usually unflappable assistant's voice, Easton entered his office and opened the inner door to store his suitcase inside. Heading directly to his desk, he sat down and opened the file.

A beautiful woman looked back at him. Not a polished headshot, this had obviously come from her social media account. Piper Townie was written in his admin's neat handwriting, along with the age of twenty-six. Easton studied her easy smile and the twinkle of happiness in her eyes. Piper sat at a table with three kids, building a ramshackle castle from multicolored plastic bricks. She looked in her element.

"Piper begins her training with me on Monday."

"I would have thought you'd allow me to choose my new admin since you're abandoning me," Easton said easily, smiling his thanks as Sharon handed him a cup of coffee made precisely as he liked it.

"Piper is perfect. You'll know it yourself when she's here for five minutes." Sharon waved away his words as she sat companionably in one chair in front of Easton's massive desk.

"I am intrigued. What made you select her?"

"She's the right one. It's time for you to find your Little girl. You weren't doing so on your own terms, so I took care of it for you."

Easton studied the incredible woman who had been his right hand for twenty years. "I think this place will fall apart without you here, Sharon."

"No way. I've got it whipped into shape now. Piper will keep it running like clockwork. She's got an impressive resume. Besides, I'll just be a phone call away. Roger needs his Mommy now and I need to be with him while he remembers," Sharon confessed before forcing a smile back to her lips.

"He's a very lucky Little to have you in his life. Roger knows that."

"Don't make me cry in the office. Let's concentrate on you. Read Piper's file and ask questions," Sharon requested as she blinked hard.

"Tell me three adjectives that you think describe her," Easton requested.

"Look at that fancy interview question you've prepared. I can't answer that for you. Keep in mind that I've only talked to her for a brief time via video conferencing. She applied for a midlevel administrative job."

"I see here she's been an executive admin for a short time. Why would she leave a higher position to apply at a lower level and pay?" Easton questioned, flipping through the pages.

"I have no proof, but I think she's escaping from something or someone."

"Never married?"

"An engagement announcement containing her name appeared in the city she lists as her home address. I asked an investigator to visit her apartment. The neighbors reported no one has seen Piper for several weeks. One saw her stuffing her car full of possessions. They assumed she'd moved in with the handsome man who they'd seen frequently at her apartment. The building's owner just listed the apartment for rent."

"And the gentleman she was dating?"

"There is a long line of restraining orders filed against him by former fiancées."

"That's not suspicious at all," Easton remarked, feeling his brows draw together in concern.

"Her application contained a note. She asked for recommendations for safe housing in the area."

"Safe housing?"

"That stood out to me as well," Sharon nodded. "After talking to her, I can confirm that her skills are top notch. Probably technically better than mine if I'm honest."

"She won't have your instincts, honed from years in this position," Easton observed.

"Not at first. But I didn't, either. My observation is she's incredibly intelligent. She wouldn't have been considered for this high of a position with her past employer without intuition and people skills. Her boss states openly in her reference letter that he's torn between speaking highly of her because she's been a phenomenal assistant and lying to tempt her back."

"Hmmm," Easton remarked as he pored over the sheets in the file. He didn't notice Sharon slipping from his office to collect her purse from her desk. Easton trusted Sharon implicitly.

Piper Townie, you intrigue me. If nothing else, I will make sure you are safe.

PART II
DADDY'S WAITING

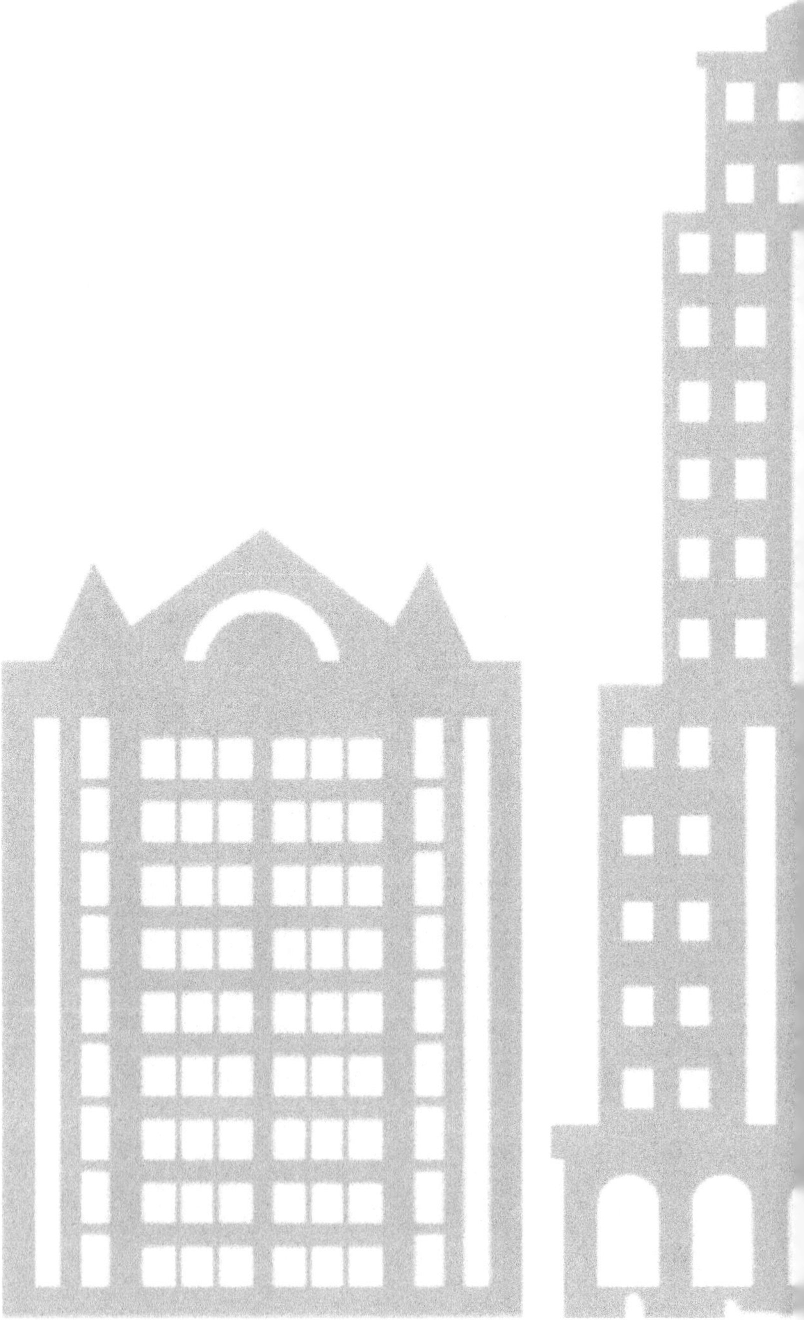

CHAPTER 1

"Ms. Townie is here, Mr. Edgewater."

"Please send her in, Sharon," Easton requested, standing and circling his desk to greet the prospective interviewee. He couldn't prevent the smile on his face as Piper Townie entered.

Dressed in a knee-length brown skirt with a copper blouse that highlighted her brown eyes, Piper looked like she had stepped out of a marketer's dream ad. Nothing flashy or eye-catching, Piper had pulled her brown hair up at the nape of her neck and wore stylish pumps with a small heel. She looked efficient and capable.

"Ms. Townie, please come in. Thank you for interviewing with me today," Easton greeted Piper.

"Mr. Edgewater, I am very glad to meet you. I must be honest, I wasn't expecting to speak to the head of the company today," Piper confessed, with a hint of a nervous tremor in her voice.

"You can thank my current administrative assistant for the change in plans. Please come in and take a seat," he encouraged.

"Thank you," she murmured politely before sitting exactly where Sharon had sat two days before.

"Sharon flagged your application for my consideration. The two of us have worked together since Edgewater Industries had been merely a dream. When she announced she needed to leave for personal reasons, Sharon decided she needed to find her replacement. So far, she has sent me exactly one applicant. You."

"That's… intriguing." Piper finished her sentence after a brief pause.

"I thought so, too. What can you tell me about yourself?" he asked, sitting back in his chair.

"I'm a dedicated employee. I work hard and am conscientious about my duties."

"Why are you leaving your present job?"

"I would like to pursue new challenges," she answered with a completely expressionless face.

"That's the first lie you've told me. Try again," he prompted.

Piper froze, and Easton could tell an internal battle had begun inside her brain. Finally, decision made, she answered, "Thank you for your time." Piper stood and held her hand out.

"One reason my company has succeeded is that I have the ability to tell when anyone is lying," Easton explained, ignoring her outstretched hand. He did not stop her as she walked toward the closed door.

Halfway there, Piper turned and looked back at him. "Anyone?"

He smiled at her inquisitive nature. "Anyone."

"That's quite a power," she answered with a twitch at one corner of her mouth.

"Try me. Tell me two true statements and a lie."

"Like the old game?" she questioned, arching one eyebrow in amusement.

"Exactly."

Piper walked forward to rest her hands on the back of the chair she'd vacated. She hesitated before ticking three statements off on her fingers. "My most prized possession is a stuffed bear. I'm afraid of the dark. I really need this job."

"True. True. True. You forgot to lie."

She stared at him in shock before shaking her head slowly. "I'm not scared of the dark."

"Someday you'll tell me the full truth. But I can wait until you trust me," Easton commented softly before changing the conversation.

"Would you come sit down and finish the interview? I think Sharon may well be right this time as she always seems to be."

"Is there anyone who can fool you?"

"No."

Piper pivoted and returned to her previous seat. "I left because I accepted the wrong man's proposal and he's sworn to never let me go. When he invaded my parents' home to leave me a message, I knew he was a threat to them as well."

"Truth once again. You need a safe place to live and work," Easton suggested.

"Yes."

He smiled inwardly as she adopted his one-word answering style. "Thank you for telling me the truth. Let me tell you how I can help you." Easton explained the benefits package he could offer her and the bonus of a small apartment in a very protected space—in the B tower of the office complex.

"Oh, employees can rent a room there?" she said in relief as she sagged against the back of the seat.

"I provide space, free of charge, for Littles who work for the company. It is my way of protecting them."

"Littles?" Piper repeated. Her hackles rose as she stared at him in disbelief. What message was she sending out that all these men kept picking up on?

"Yes."

"Like children?" she asked, trying to lead the conversation in another direction. "Isn't that against the law?"

"No, I only employ those eighteen or older here. My suspicion is that you have known you're a Little for a long time. I take it from your defensive posture that your former fiancé called himself a Daddy?"

Piper stared at him in shock. *How does he know all of this?*

"Not all who call themselves Daddies have the caring, nurturing capacity that role demands. Some pervert that title to take away a Little's power. Never allow anyone to do that."

Finding herself unable to lie to him for something other than the simple reason he would immediately know, Piper clutched at the situation. "I prefer to keep my private life and my career separated."

Piper's mind raced as she tried to digest his word. *Pervert. Are there Daddies who don't use their Little's fantasies for their gain?*

Mentally, she shook her head to concentrate on the man before her. Forcing her hands to relax in her lap, she tried not to give away any secrets to this extremely observant man. To her relief, he shifted the conversation.

"Understandable. If you would like, Sharon will give you a tour of the apartment available before you train with her," Easton suggested.

Tensing, she curbed her body's instant reaction to his gentle smile. Why was she responding so quickly to this man's acceptance? Forcing herself back into proper interview demeanor, she asked, shell-shocked, "That's it? You're hiring me to be your administrative assistant?"

"If you would like the job, it is yours. I think we would work well together. Sharon will stay on for one week to assist in the transition. Then she has offered to be a phone call away if you need her."

"Yes. That sounds amazing. I'll take the job, thank you." She smiled at her new employer, feeling relief flood her body. *Please let this be the answer I've searched for! Let me be safe here.*

"You are very welcome, Piper. Welcome to the Edgewater Industries family."

A jingle at the door drew both of their attention. "I have the key to apartment five eleven. It's available tonight. Let's take a walk, Piper," Sharon suggested.

"O-Okay." Piper stumbled at the fast pace of her life changing. Standing, she looked back at Easton Edgewater. "Thank you, sir. I'll work very hard to be, if not the best assistant you've ever had," she paused, looking at Sharon before meeting her new boss' gaze, "at least an extremely strong second place."

"I will see you later this afternoon." He accepted her promise with a nod.

Piper followed Sharon out of the office and to a different elevator than she had ridden up that morning. Sharon fit a small key on the ring she held into a slot and the door opened immediately. As they stepped in the mirror-lined car, Sharon pushed the button labeled L. Piper noticed that there were only three: T, L, E. She quickly translated Lobby and Easton, correcting herself to Mr. Edgewater.

Forcing her mind away from the mesmerizing man, she asked, "What does T stand for?"

"Tunnel. This is the key to Mr. Edgewater's private elevator. You are not to invite anyone else to ride with you—other than Mr. Edgewater, of course."

"I understand," Piper murmured as she thought, "A private elevator?"

The doors opened to a quiet corridor and Sharon gestured at the glass exterior doors a few steps away. "Outside those doors is Mr. Edgewater's parking spot. Your parking spot will be next to his if you ever need it. Most days, I bet you'll choose to walk across the grounds from your apartment in B tower to this A building. Let me show you how you can avoid bad weather or if it's dark. We'll come back by the outdoor path."

"Will I need to be on call twenty-four hours a day?" Piper asked in concern.

"No, you need only work from eight to five with an hour lunch break. If, however, you wish to arrive early or leave late, this is another option for you," Sharon answered smoothly as she pressed the T button. "We do have torrential rain and a trace of snow from time to time."

The elevator opened to reveal a brightly lit vestibule feeding into a passageway to their left. Sharon beckoned her into the tunnel and set a quick pace to the next building. Along the brightly colored walls, pictures of the history of Edgewater Industries hung along with highlighted employees from the many departments that filled the three towers. The impression was that the company treasured its employees.

Everything kept turning out better than she'd dreamed. Piper was glad she had comfortable shoes. The tunnel was longer than she expected between buildings. Walking underneath one massive tower to another gave her a greater feeling of their size. Finally, they came to another wide opening. A painted 'B' on the wall announced their destination.

"Here's your new home. Normally, you'll need to put the pink key in the elevator and press your forefinger to the reader. We'll put you in the system when we reach your new apartment. I'll press my finger instead this time. We'll double-check that everything works before we leave," Sharon reassured her.

"Thank you. The security here is quite extensive."

"It is. Mr. Edgewater protects his employees. Especially in this building."

Before Piper could ask why this building in particular, the elevator doors opened and the women stepped inside. Sharon inserted the key again and pushed the fifth floor button. The car moved smoothly upward as Piper watched the numbers flash as they rose.

"Here we are. Your new apartment is five eleven. It's to the right." Sharon led the way.

"I didn't ask if you preferred a furnished or unfurnished apartment. This one has the basic furniture inside. If that doesn't work for you, I can move you to an empty one," Sharon assured her as she opened the door with the gilded numbers 511.

"It's lovely," Piper said in amazement as she looked around the small apartment. The first large room was open with a kitchen in one corner and living space filling the others. A large, overstuffed couch and chair invited her to come sit down and relax. The kitchen island separated the cooking space and, while small, even had a dishwasher, to her surprise.

Without waiting for Sharon, Piper walked to the hallway. To the left was a bathroom with a tub/shower combination. She peeked behind a set of louvered doors and found a stacked washer and dryer. To the right, the bedroom beckoned. It had a large bed with a railing at each side of the headboard that seemed to roll into the wall. Tearing her eyes away, she noted the immense dresser with a padded top and no mirror. Perhaps the last resident had a destructive cat?

"I've never seen a queen-sized bed with a railing around it," Piper mused. She tugged the edge by the nightstand. It glided down the side of the bed. Piper pushed it back into the wall to allow herself access to the interior of the bed.

"A new safety feature," Sharon commented smoothly.

Piper sat in the immense chair by the window. "It's a rocker. I'll love to sit here and read," she mentioned.

"Perfect. You'll love the light that streams in this side. There are office buildings beside the apartment, so be sure to close your windows," Sharon cautioned.

"Good reminder. I must admit I'm amazed by this apartment. I had been living on my parents' farm recently. This is completely different." Piper tried to keep her tone light but knew her eyes shone with tears when she thought of Gabriel having those she loved as possible targets.

"I'm glad you found your way to Edgewater. Perhaps a new beginning is just the thing you need," Sharon remarked softly.

"Thank you. Is it okay if I move my suitcases in tonight? I can start work now. I know I only have you around for a week," Piper asked, eager to get started.

"Let's get your fingerprint in the apartment system and we'll walk back to the main building by the outdoor path." Sharon led her over to a pad by the door. She typed a few strange letter combinations and a green glowing fingertip appeared.

"Press whichever finger from either hand on the pad. I always advise your non-dominant hand. That's usually the one you use to carry something. This way you don't have to juggle."

Piper stepped up to the glowing display and pressed her left thumb to the screen. She stepped back when Sharon approached again. Watching over the other woman's shoulder, Piper jumped when the screen flashed to red.

"Now, press a finger that you want to use as an alert that something is wrong," Sharon instructed.

"Is this a dangerous neighborhood?" Piper blurted apprehensively.

"No. It's incredibly safe here. There are guards at the entrances and security patrols on the grounds. Our highly classified contracts require heightened entry screening. More important, Mr. Edgewater wishes to ensure everyone's well-being. You'll find he takes care of his employees. Easton lives here himself."

"Really? In this building?"

"No, his apartment is attached to his office so he can easily go back and forth if needed. Now, choose a finger you'd never naturally press against the screen," Sharon encouraged.

Piper stepped back to the screen and carefully pressed her middle fingertip to the screen. At the sound of Sharon's laugh, she looked over her shoulder to see the other woman's relaxed expression. "It seemed appropriate?" she said with a shrug.

"Mine is exactly the same finger. I think we're going to get along fine. Great minds and all of that! Come on. Let's go get started. You've got a lot to pick up."

Sharon handed her the keys and opened the door. When Piper had relocked it, she led the way back to the elevator. As they reached the elevator, a plump blonde emerged through a nearby door marked STAIRS.

"Hi, Regina. This is Piper. She's moving in after work."

"Hi, Piper. Welcome! I'm in five twenty-three if you need anything or just want to chat. Everyone is super friendly here. I'm off to pick up something for Mr. Walker that I left in my apartment. Knock if you need some help getting stuff upstairs. I'm trying to lose a few pounds." Regina gestured at the stairs.

"I could use some exercise, too," Piper laughed. "But after I lug everything upstairs."

"Good plan!" With a wave, Regina rushed down the corridor.

Reassured that she'd have at least one friendly person on the floor, Piper smiled to herself. She'd loved seeing Sharon smile, too. It seemed she had a nonprofessional side as well.

Riding to the lobby this time in the elevator, Sharon had her practice using her fingerprint and her key to make sure it worked. Like magic, pressing her fingertip to the screen called for the doors to open. Sharon waved her across the lobby and stopped to introduce her to the guard sitting at the large reception area just inside the doors.

"Piper, you're in luck. You get to meet our head of security. This is

Knox Miller," Sharon said, smiling at the enormous man behind the counter.

"Hi, Piper!" His voice was low and gravelly, the perfect match for the muscled man. He hit a few keys on the computer and looked at her. "You're staying in apartment five eleven and working for Mr. Edgewater. Hold still for a photo."

He paused for a few seconds as she processed his words. When she smiled automatically for a photo, he lifted a small eyeball camera. "Thank you, Piper. I'll process your ID badge and have it here at the desk after work. If you have things to move into your apartment, ask at the desk for help. We always have powerful guys around to help."

"Thank you, Knox. I appreciate the help. I'll be sure to talk to the attendant here at the desk."

"My pleasure. That's what I do around here. I'm sure we'll run into each other frequently," he said, stroking his thick black beard.

Piper nodded and turned to look at Sharon. She felt like he knew all about her. Not much would escape the sharp eyes of the security head.

"Shall we continue the tour?" Piper asked.

"If you'll excuse us, Knox, we'll be on our way." Sharon stepped away with a wave.

"Of course. See you soon, Piper."

CHAPTER 2

Piper pressed her finger against the elevator's electronic pad and turned the key. She was exhausted. Needing to unpack her car, she barely had enough energy to go upstairs to double-check that she could actually get into the beautiful apartment before crashing. Did she need anything from the car that couldn't wait for tomorrow? Running her tongue over her teeth, Piper knew she wouldn't be able to sleep without brushing her teeth.

"Piper, we're ready to help unload your car. Want to just give us the keys and we'll unload everything?"

The vaguely familiar voice made her look around. The security guy, Knox, stood behind her. His size made her shrink against the wall. Instantly, he backed up. Signaling the guys behind him to disperse, Knox deliberately lowered his open hands down to his sides.

"Piper, I'm never going to hurt you. I'm here to keep the bad guys out. I can tell you're exhausted."

"I'm sorry, Knox. Of course you're not going to hurt me. I'd love your help," Piper said, making herself stand straight. She felt awful. He had not given her one reason to be scared.

"Would you like to take a seat down here and we'll just pile everything in the middle of the main room? Maybe put your suitcase on the bed?" he asked quietly.

"That would be amazing. Let me pull my car around. It's in the visitor's parking lot," Piper said, allowing him to see the relief in her gaze.

"Pete is a skilled driver. Give him your keys and he'll take care of it," Knox suggested. He motioned for a smaller, wiry man to come forward.

Immediately, Piper dug in her purse for her keys. Handing them to Pete, she said, "Thank you, Pete. My car is a beige sedan with out-of-state license plates. It's parked in front of the fountain."

"Got it. We'll handle it for you," Pete promised with a smile.

Knox gestured toward the comfortable seating area in the reception area. He allowed her to pick a seat and sat down across from her. Pulling out his phone, Knox pressed a few places on his screen before looking at her. "Your ex-fiancé is Gabriel Serrano from Argentina. He's six feet two inches tall with black hair and brown eyes. He does not have a police record. You fear he will find you here."

Piper looked at him. She closed her mouth when she realized that it had dropped open in surprise. "You investigated me?"

"I do a background check on every employee. The results of the screening stay with me in a file. I do not share the information unless it becomes necessary for your safety."

"I'm afraid he's coming for me. Would you like me to leave?"

"No. My job is to keep everyone safe. Edgewater is a company focused on creating a safe place for everyone. Your ex will not get through our safety protocol. I need you to tell me if you hear from him or even have an inkling that he's found you," Knox requested firmly.

Nodding at the large man, Piper was super sorry that she'd ever reacted in fear toward him. This man was not an enemy. He was her best defense.

"I'm very lucky to have gotten a job here."

"Mr. Edgewater wouldn't have hired you if he didn't know you were perfect for the job," Knox firmly stated.

"Thank you," she said, smiling at him for the first time. A group of people walked into the tower. One carried a large brown stuffed monkey. His arms barely fit around the stuffie's waist. Instantly, Piper wanted to know how squishy he was.

"Hi, Knox!" they greeted the large man.

"Hi, Littles. This is Piper. She's moving in on the fifth floor. Introduce yourselves," Knox directed as they flopped into the surrounding chairs.

One word of his greeting stuck in her head. Littles? The only definition she could give that was the one from her books. Those e-books that she devoured on her reader. That couldn't be what he was talking about, could it? She'd tried to convince herself that Mr. Edgewater hadn't really identified her as a Little.

Thankfully, it looked like her tough conversation with Knox was finished. Piper relaxed against the padded back and smiled at the newcomers. Three men entered with their arms full. Knowing that they carried her belongings to the elevator, Piper scooted to the edge of the cushion to stand. At Knox's headshake, she slid back fully on the sofa and relaxed. They would handle it.

By this time, the new arrivals had all recited their names and smiled at her. Quickly, she babbled, "Hi, everyone. I'm sorry. My mind couldn't focus. Could you do that again?"

They all laughed and cheerfully repeated themselves.

"I'm Tess."

"I'm Danny and this is Mono. That's Spanish for monkey," he explained.

"Alan."

"Terri."

"I'm Yuri. I just started my job here a month ago. It's a great place. Don't worry if you don't remember our names. It's tough getting a new job and moving. We'll remind you," a chipper man answered.

"Thanks." Piper loved how they ranged in age from early twenties to mid-forties, she guessed. All seemed to feel right at home. Tentatively, she stretched a hand out to touch Mono's fur, stopping an inch away for permission from Danny. When he nodded, she stroked the stuffie's foot. She smiled at the feel of the soft fur.

"I'm glad to meet all of you, including Sr. Mono. Where do you all work?"

"Building A."

"Building A."

"Building C."

"Building A."

"Building C. Where are you?"

"Building A. I'm working for Mr. Edgewater."

"I bet he's a great boss."

"That's got to be a hard job. He's super busy!" Alan guessed.

"I have a lot to learn," Piper nodded in agreement.

Everyone chatted, getting to know each other. It seemed like in a flash Pete brought the keys back to Piper. He handed them to her with a smile.

"Everything's unpacked. I parked your car just outside the door to the left. It's locked for the night."

"Thank you, Pete. Please thank the others for me." Piper fumbled with the latch on her purse to find her wallet to tip the men. Tess, sitting on her right, put her hand on Piper's knee and shook her head. Immediately, Piper stilled.

When Pete stepped away, Tess leaned over to whisper into her ear, "That's not needed here. They want to take care of us." She nodded as Pete dragged Alan to his feet and sat down in his place, pulling the grown man onto his lap. To Piper's surprise, Alan melted against Pete.

"Pete is Alan's Daddy. He'd want others to take care of Alan, just like they helped you," Tess explained. "Do you have a Daddy?"

"No," Piper answered, without thinking first about what she revealed.

"It's okay. He'll find you," Tess said confidently.

"Pizza was just delivered to the guard shack," Pete announced. "They're bringing it over now. Who doesn't have anything for dinner tonight?"

Tess, Danny, Alan, Terri, and Yuri all raised their hands. Danny lifted Mono's paw as well. They looked at Piper.

"I haven't run to the store. I wasn't expecting to find a job, an apartment, and friends the first day," Piper admitted.

"There will be lots of pizzas. Stay and have dinner with us!" Danny urged.

"Pizza is my favorite food. If you don't mind, I'd love to join you!"

A buff man in a uniform appeared carrying a stack of pizza boxes and bottles of chilled water. "These are courtesy of Mr. Edgewater. I bet you're Piper," he said, meeting her gaze.

When she nodded, he continued, "I was to take one of the cheese pizzas to your room if you weren't here. Mr. Edgewater will be glad to hear you've blended in already."

With a nod of his head at her and then acknowledging Knox's presence, he turned and headed back to the security point. In the flurry of everyone opening boxes and choosing a slice of their favorites, Piper mulled over how Mr. Edgewater was taking care of her. She hated the negative worries that immediately popped into her head.

"How much is the rent here?" she asked Tess quietly. The sweet woman had become her informational source already. Mr. Edgewater had told her that there was no charge, but she wanted to confirm that.

"Rent? Oh, it's free here. Mr. Edgewater takes care of his employees," Tess reassured her.

"Really?"

"Really. He knows employees can concentrate and work better when they aren't worried about the basic stuff in life like shelter and food." Tess motioned with her pizza slice at the display before them. "Mr. Edgewater truly cares about everyone who works here."

"This place seems ideal. What's the negative parts?" Piper asked quietly.

Danny overheard the soft whisperers and answered for Tess, "There aren't any. If you do your job, you're set. If you don't, Mr. Edgewater doesn't mess around. You lose all this."

"I enjoy working," Piper rushed to assure them.

"Eat, Littles," Knox directed from the other side of the gathering as he picked up a second slice of pizza. "I'm going to eat it all before you finish your first piece."

A wave of laughter wafted from the assembled group as they munched and chatted. It had been so long since Piper had hung around with people in a fun social setting. She soaked in all the cheerful conversations and found she was learning a lot just listening.

Soon, the pieces in the boxes dwindled, seemingly taking everyone's energy with them.

Pete boosted Alan up to his feet. "Time for bed, young man. You're grumpy if you don't have enough sleep."

Alan's face turned faintly pink in the bright fluorescent lighting. He didn't argue, but took Pete's hand and walked to the elevator to activate it.

Piper rose to her feet. "Thanks for letting me share the pizza, but most of all, thanks for making my first night here almost a party. I'm going to head up to my apartment to make sure I've got things ready for tomorrow. Thank you, Knox, for asking the staff to unload my car."

"All you have to do is ask. We're glad to help," the large man answered with a smile.

A few minutes later, Piper opened her new apartment door and stepped inside, expecting to see a mess waiting. To her surprise, the apartment looked almost as pristine as it had when she'd visited earlier. They had neatly stacked her sparse possessions against the small dining nook wall, completely out of the way. Piper turned and locked the door behind her with a sigh of relief.

She had brought only the things most precious to her. Her plan to get household items later would work perfectly here. Piper could easily order sheets and towels online. Family pictures and mementos of those closest to her rested securely in the few boxes she'd fit into her car. Piper ran her hand over the container labeled 'family pictures.'

Realizing she hadn't updated her parents, Piper pulled out her phone and texted them a message. *I made it here, guys. I got the job and an apartment inside the grounds. Super safe here.*

Exhausted, Piper headed to the bedroom to figure out what she needed to do before crashing into bed. To her surprise, a lamp on the nightstand softly illuminated the beautiful room. The soft puddle of light spilled over crisp sheets that someone had turned down invitingly. With a groan of delight, Piper ran her hand over the soft bedding.

She turned to her suitcase resting on the dresser and quickly unzipped it. Lifting a well-loved teddy bear from his bed of clothing, Piper hugged her best friend in the world. "I think we're safe here, Stanley. No more hiding in suitcases," she promised.

When Stanley seemed reassured, Piper set him gently on the pillow. She shook out the two dressier outfits and hung them in the closet to release a few of the wrinkles overnight. Grabbing her nightshirt, Piper walked to the bathroom, hoping that the kind people who had turned down her bed had also left a towel and soap. To her delight, the bathroom was completely stocked. A quick peek into the closet revealed a stack of towels and washcloths as well as shampoo, deodorant, soap, and even toilet paper.

Sending a mental thank you to her fairy godmother or whoever was so thoughtful, Piper quickly stripped. She neatly stowed her clothes in the hamper before looking yearningly at the large tub. That would have to wait for another day. Quickly showering and dressing in her nightshirt, Piper felt almost human as she turned off all the lights but the bathroom. The glow coming down the hall offset the pitch-black darkness.

Unable to resist the need to double-check, she peeked at the front door to make sure the chain was in place. After plugging in her phone and setting an alarm, Piper slid under the covers and pulled Stanley close. Instantly, she crashed into the first deep sleep since the farm's invasion.

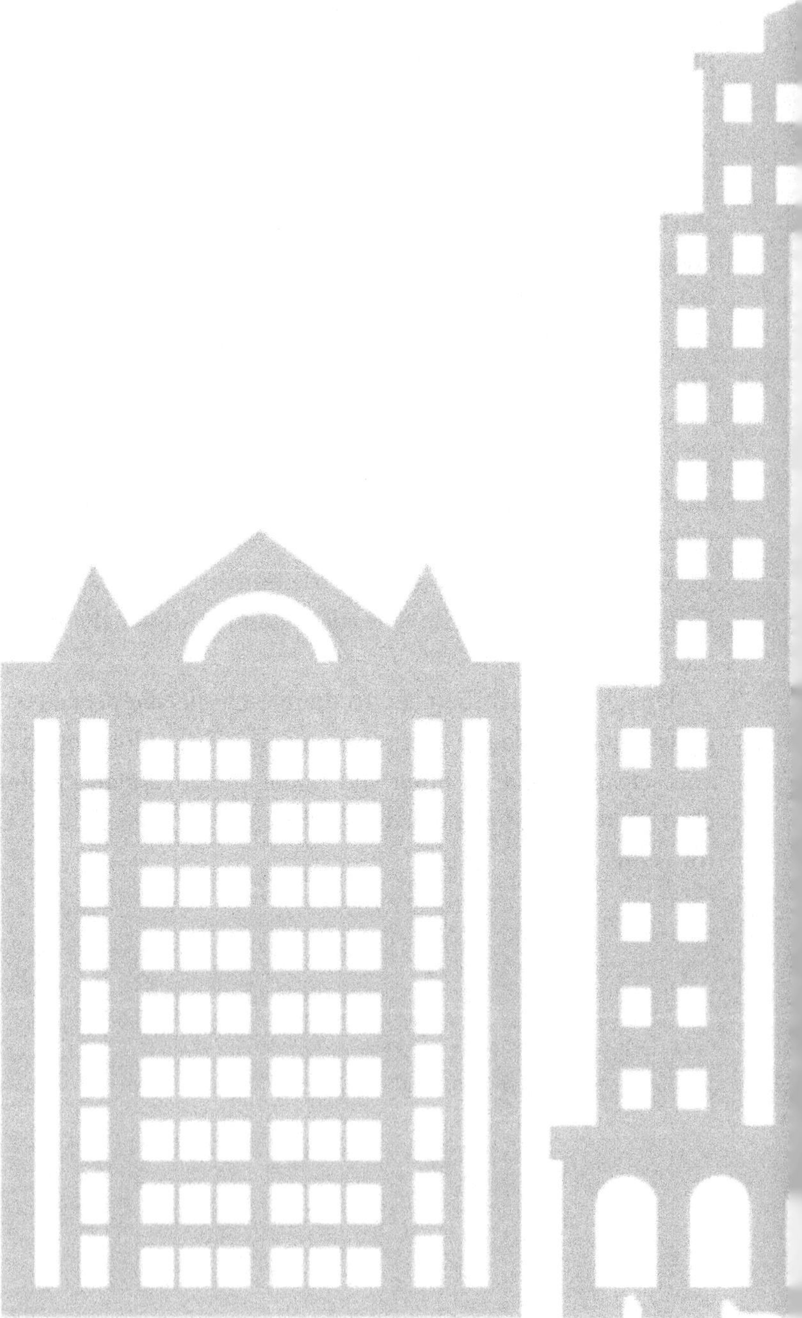

CHAPTER 3

Mechanical beeping jarred Piper from a bad dream. She jackknifed into a sitting position in the middle of the bed as she looked around, breathing heavily. The unfamiliar bedroom added to her distress. Hugging Stanley to her chest, Piper forced herself to calm her breathing and settle her frantically beating heart.

"I'm safe. He can't get me. I'm safe." She repeated the words that had become her mantra in recent days.

Finally, Piper felt her heart rate slow. Catching sight of the time, she kissed Stanley's head softly and placed him on the pillow. She scooted out of bed and smoothed the covers around his shoulders. "There. You rest from the trip while I'm gone, Stanley."

Dashing into the bathroom, she cleaned up, transforming herself back into the polished administrative assistant. Piper selected the least wrinkled of her hanging office clothes and dressed. A quick look in the mirror reassured her that Mr. Edgewater would not detect her morning panic attack.

Grabbing her keys and phone, Piper hesitated when her stomach growled. On a hunch, she entered the small galley kitchen and opened the refrigerator. A variety of staples and fresh fruit and vegetables looked back at her. Piper opened the drawer to select a shiny red apple. She washed it quickly and took a bite.

"Mmm." She hummed in appreciation of the crisp fruit. With a smile, Piper let herself out of the apartment and headed to the elevator. Cheerful people greeted her as she crossed the lobby and took the outside path to building A.

It was a glorious day. Gorgeous flowers lined the path, their fragrance surrounding her. Piper paused to take a deep breath to enjoy them before lifting her chin into the morning light. The sunshine felt good on her face. The stress of the last few days seemed to melt away in this beautiful haven. Smiling, she bit into her crunchy apple and continued on her way, eager to start the day.

A few minutes later, she stepped out of the private elevator to find Sharon stowing her purse in the desk drawer. "Good morning," Piper called cheerfully. She'd enjoyed working closely with Sharon yesterday. The experienced employee had shared a myriad of tips from her years of experience. "I'll just toss this in the trash and wash my hands."

"Good morning, Piper. You're an early bird like me. Grab a cup of coffee on your way back if you'd like," Sharon suggested.

"Thanks," Piper answered with a smile. Quickly, she got rid of the apple core and cleaned the sticky juice off her hands. Exploring, she found an array of coffee pods and filled up the water tank before pushing the button. As she waited, Piper noted the water bottles stocked in the see-through fridge and suspected they would be fair game as well. Picking up her cup, she headed back to the huge desk.

"Sharon, could you bring in coffee, please?" Mr. Edgewater's voice came through the open door.

"He likes it black with a squirt of honey," Sharon informed her. "Why don't you take it inside to him and say good morning."

Nodding, Piper set her cup down and hurried to brew another. After adding a generous squeeze of the honey bear on the counter, she carefully carried it into her new boss' office. She hesitated upon seeing the panel of brightly lit monitors revealing a half dozen faces.

"Good morning, Piper," he greeted her before holding up one finger to signal a quick break. Without waiting to see their responses, Mr. Edgewater pressed a button and turned from the now darkened screens to smile at her.

"I'm sorry to interrupt. Here's your coffee, sir." Piper set the warm coffee mug on the corner of his desk.

"I'm glad to see you this morning. I hope you slept well."

"I did. Thank you."

The two looked at each other for a couple of seconds before Piper rushed to fill the silence. "Thank you for the pizza party last night. I enjoyed meeting a few of the other employees that live in B tower."

"My pleasure. I'm glad you're making friends and settling in. I must get back to my meeting, but I wanted to ask if you would come to lunch with me today. I'd like to get to know you better," he requested.

"I'd like that."

"Truth. I'm glad."

Easton's smile warmed her. She felt like they had a connection already. Pulling herself together, Piper asked, "Shall I tell Sharon as well?"

"No, Sharon has plans with her husband today. She's only working a half day today."

"I better go ask lots of questions then," Piper said with a smile, backing out of the office.

"Close the door, Piper. We'll have lunch at one."

As she stepped out of the room, pulling the large wooden door into place, Piper saw the screens relight. Mr. Edgewater slid back into the conversation. As the door snicked closed, she smiled to herself. Piper was sure he was just being nice to take her to lunch, but it meant a lot that he wanted to get to know her better.

Returning to the desk, she found Sharon ready to explain the spreadsheets they'd left last night. "Okay, before we start with the new information, can I review what we talked about with these records yesterday?"

"Good idea. Ask any questions you have," Sharon suggested.

Piper turned back one page on the yellow pad of paper she'd used for notes. Running through the last information, she paused. "I know I'm supposed to submit these to Accounting. Do I have a contact in Accounting who receives these?"

"Definitely, his name is Barry Mattson. I had the tech department bring a laptop for you to use." Sharon reached into the desk and pulled out a sleek machine. "Let's get you logged in and then you can save all your contacts."

The two women dove back into her training. Piper continued to take careful notes as she tried to absorb all the information Sharon walked her through. Her head was swimming after two hours. When someone rapped loudly on the open door, she looked up with relief at the interruption.

"Sharon, I need to talk to Easton immediately." The brusque woman walked directly to his closed office door.

Sharon drew Piper's attention to a button at the corner of the large desk. Pushing it quickly, she greeted the employee, "Hi, Ms. Rivers. Unfortunately, Mr. Edgewater is in a meeting that will last all morning."

The woman tested the doorknob and found it locked. "This is important, Sharon. I need to talk to Easton now."

"I understand. I can only go by his directions. I know he's screening messages. Have you tried emailing him?"

"Of course. He's not answering."

"He will. Give him some time," Sharon suggested.

"When he emerges, ask him to contact me."

"Will do!" Sharon answered cheerfully.

When the woman rushed from the room, Sharon shared, "That's Elaine Rivers. She is Easton's second in command and has an absolutely brilliant business mind."

Piper added that to her list of contacts with a brief note. "No one interrupts Mr. Edgewater?"

"When his door is closed, do not interrupt him unless there is a major emergency, something along the lines of a total business evacuation," she added for clarification. "If his door is open, then it is safe to contact him with the name of the visitor. I usually send him a message."

"And you have the ability to lock his door to keep out the most persistent visitors?" Piper asked, leaning toward the corner of the desk to see there were actually two buttons. "What's the second one for?"

"That calls security. I've never used it. No one gets past the security gate at the entrance. It's special protection for his office. Mr. Edgewater put it in to make sure I was safe. Let's get out of the office for a while. We'll visit some other offices so I can introduce you to the people we've discussed in those key positions."

Sharon walked Piper around the key offices in A building. Taking careful notes, Piper noticed Sharon didn't always visit the people whose names were in the biggest letters on the door. The administrative assistant had obviously created her own list of most important employees. They visited several floors, giving Piper an opportunity to look around as well. To her delight, she ran into Tess and Alan. They greeted her with hugs and seemed genuinely happy to see her.

"Ready for C building?" Sharon asked with a smile.

"Sure. Isn't there anything important in B building?"

"The most important people are in B building," Sharon shared. "The security offices are also there, and you've met Knox already. His department is all Daddies. It goes along with the territory, I guess."

"My ex-fiancé was a Daddy, too," Piper blurted, not too reassured by Sharon's words.

"I would guess that the man you were smart enough to run far away from used the title of Daddy to cover up for very un-Daddy-like behavior."

"Are there really that many Daddies and Littles out there?" Piper asked as they walked through the bright sunlight to the far building.

"Yes."

"Can I ask you something personal? Feel free to tell me no," Piper rushed to add.

"Go ahead and ask. I'll reserve the right to not answer if I don't want to," Sharon answered.

"That's fair. Are you a Little?"

"Ten years ago, I would have answered yes. A bratty Little on top of that!" Sharon laughed. "Life has a way of muddying things up. My husband suffers from early onset dementia. Our roles have flip-flopped."

"I'm sorry. That was a very personal question to ask," Piper rushed to apologize.

"It's okay. You've run into a lot of Littles here. It's only natural that you question the roles people have in their lives. Edgewater Industries is a very inclusive company. Each employee is encouraged to live their best life—whatever that life entails. They protect Littles here most of all."

"Because Mr. Edgewater has been looking for his Little?" Piper asked.

"No. Because Littles have a special place in his heart."

Their entrance into C building interrupted their conversation. Piper looked around, noting this tower also had its own vibe that differed from the corporate feel of A and the homey feel of B. Here, she absorbed an efficient industrial feel. There was less glitz and glamour and more quiet expertise. The real work seemed to happen here.

She followed Sharon to the desk and checked in with her new ID badge. The security guard scanned the barcode on the back before returning it.

"What floor are you visiting today, ladies?" he asked.

"We're going to the third and fourth," Sharon answered.

The guard punched a few buttons and gave the okay. "Elevator 4 will take you to the third floor. Please use it to reach the fourth floor and to return to the lobby."

As they walked to the bank of elevators, only one was lit. The doors slid open as they approached. The others sat still and silent. Inside, two numbers glowed on the panel. Obviously, the guard had allowed them access only to the floors Sharon requested. Access to the other areas was restricted.

Sharon said nothing until the door closed. "As Mr. Edgewater's admin, you will have access to almost any area in all three buildings. Here, I have chosen only to visit the third and fourth floors. The other floors have top-secret projects going or other sensitive departments. The third floor is accounting and the fourth floor is technology."

"Those sound like good departments to have a contact in," Piper agreed with a nod.

"Technology will come to you if there's a problem with a computer or the functioning of the communication tools that Mr. Edgewater uses regularly."

"Oh, like the wall of screens I saw earlier," Piper chimed in.

"Exactly. There are times that having a friend in the tech center is a definite bonus. I'll introduce you to Belinda first. She's scary smart and equally personable," Sharon said.

Quickly, Piper jotted her name down in her notebook. She'd need to organize her notes to use them efficiently. Piper decided tonight would be a good time to get that process underway. *Heavens knows I don't have anything else pressing to do.*

When the elevator door glided open, Sharon led her down a tiled hallway to an open area of cubicles. They walked past rows of tech people focused on multiple screens in front of them, with earphones plugged in. A few here and there talked quietly on the phone, leading callers through helpline protocols. Piper was glad she no longer manned a desk in an administrative assistants' pool.

"Belinda is in the far corner. I ran into her at a social event for the company a few years back. She's worked her way up the ladder and could have her own office, but she prefers to be with the others." Sharon turned at the end of the row and entered a large cube with a stunning blonde frowning at a document on the screen.

Expecting Belinda to be masking the hubbub around her also, Piper murmured, "Looks like we've come at the wrong time."

To her surprise, the woman immediately looked up with a smile. "You're here at a great time. I've grimaced at that report long enough. Hi, Sharon!" She stood to shake hands with them both.

"I bet you're Piper. I'll admit I'm intrigued to meet you. Sharon's a legend around here. I can't imagine stepping into her shoes."

"Piper will fit in seamlessly here," Sharon smoothly assured Belinda.

"Hi, Belinda. I'll admit I'm a bit intimidated but determined to do a great job. It's nice to have experts to call on." Piper smiled at the friendly woman.

"Belinda is a great resource for speeding up the process for tech requests and needs. I contacted her for your computer and it arrived in less than an hour," Sharon told her.

"There's no need for a computer to sit on the shelf when someone needs to work." Belinda dismissed her prompt response. "Let me give you my cell number. That way you can contact me whenever you need to. Fair warning, I may not respond immediately but I will get back to you."

"Of course. Thank you." Piper pulled out her phone and froze.

Where have you run, Little girl? I will find you!

Trying to cover her fright, Piper swiped her finger over the screen to dismiss the message. She pulled up her contacts and entered Belinda's name. "Ready," she announced.

Quickly, Belinda read off her phone number. Piper entered and saved it before dialing it. "You'll have my number as well. If I can return the favor and help you sometime, let me know."

"Thank you, Piper." Belinda hesitated before asking, "Are you okay? All the color just bleached from your face."

"I'm great. Thank you for being concerned," Piper smiled as she tried to cover up her reaction.

"We won't take any more of your time, Belinda. Thank you for meeting with us. I'll miss chatting with you." Sharon smiled at her contact.

"Come back and visit. I'd love to stay in touch."

Sharon nodded and shepherded Piper out of the cubicle. "One more person to meet and we'll finish just in time for your lunch with Mr. Edgewater."

When they reached elevator four, it again opened for them. Floor three glowed from the panel. Sharon pressed the button and set the car in motion.

"I want you to show that message to Knox," she said softly.

Piper looked at her in surprise. "Why would I do that?"

"Knox is the head of security. You should update him anytime your ex-fiancé contacts you."

"I don't want to bring my personal problems to work."

"You're part of the Edgewater family now and live here on the grounds, Piper. You don't want to endanger anyone else," Sharon assured her quietly as they stepped onto the thick carpet of the next floor. "Knox needs to know."

Piper nodded before following Sharon down the hall. She hadn't thought of it that way. Her thoughts raced through her mind. It was important to protect everyone. She didn't think Gabriel would hurt anyone else. Frankly, she'd hoped he would leave her alone now that she couldn't help his underhanded acts at her last company. Lost in thought, she almost bumped into Sharon when she stopped abruptly.

"Hi, Barry! Let me introduce Mr. Edgewater's new admin. This is Piper Townie."

"You found your replacement, huh?" the older man said with a smile. "I'm glad to meet you, Piper."

"Barry has been with Edgewater Industries for a long time," she explained to Piper before turning back to chat with Barry.

"I think I only have about three months' seniority on you," Sharon said with a laugh.

"Two and a half," he said with a serious expression that morphed into an answering laugh, as if he couldn't keep a straight face for too long. "When you leave, only Mr. Edgewater will have been working for the company longer than me."

"Barry looks harmless, but he's the gatekeeper for all the company's funds. Nothing gets spent without his okay," Sharon confided to Piper.

"I've learned that we waste a lot of money on stupid stuff. I'm glad to be the roadblock to all the worthless things," Barry explained. "Mr. Edgewater is counting on me."

"Sounds like he's lucky you're here," Piper commented in amazement. Not many people were so dedicated to protecting their company.

"Oh, I get my rewards. Mr. Edgewater is a smart man. A gift from many years ago, I own a small percentage of the company. By saving him money, I make myself money."

"Don't let him fool you, Piper. Inside that brain is the workings of a mastermind accountant," Sharon said.

"I count on Sharon for her insight working with Mr. Edgewater. I hope I can ask for your opinion as well?" he asked Piper.

"I definitely won't know as much as Sharon, but I'll always give you my impressions," Piper promised.

"That's all I can ask. Thank you, Piper. I'm glad we've met."

"Bye, old friend. I'll see you soon, I'm sure," Sharon assured her long-time colleague.

"The best of all to you. When it's time, come back."

Piper's gaze jumped to Sharon's face, trying to read her expression. Had Easton hired her for a short time? She quietly followed the woman charged with training her. When they were once again in the elevator, Piper watched the display, unsure what to say.

"I won't return to my position as Easton's admin. That position is now yours," Sharon said softly, instantly drawing Piper's gaze.

"I'm sure he would want you back. You've been with him forever." Piper voiced the worry inside her mind.

"Easton has another position in mind for me. I'll take that one when it's time. I chose you as my permanent replacement for a reason. You'll understand as you settle into your new job."

Piper nodded as she struggled to understand. The two women walked through the beautiful sunlight back to building A and Piper's lunch with her new boss. With each step, her nervousness built. Already, this morning had not gone as she'd planned. Between Gabriel's message and the shock that Sharon planned to return at some point, Piper felt like the ground underneath her was riddled with sinkholes. Her confidence in her new job and home wavered.

Sharon stopped and placed her hand softly on Piper's arm. "Truly. Your job belongs to you. I've done all I can for Easton as his admin. It's past time for me to move on."

Exhaling audibly, Piper felt her shoulders relax down into place. She nodded at the other woman. "Thanks. I shouldn't feel so settled here already, but I really want to do well in this job."

"Come on. Let's get you to lunch. You'll need to build some insight into your new boss to work efficiently with him. That starts with spending time together."

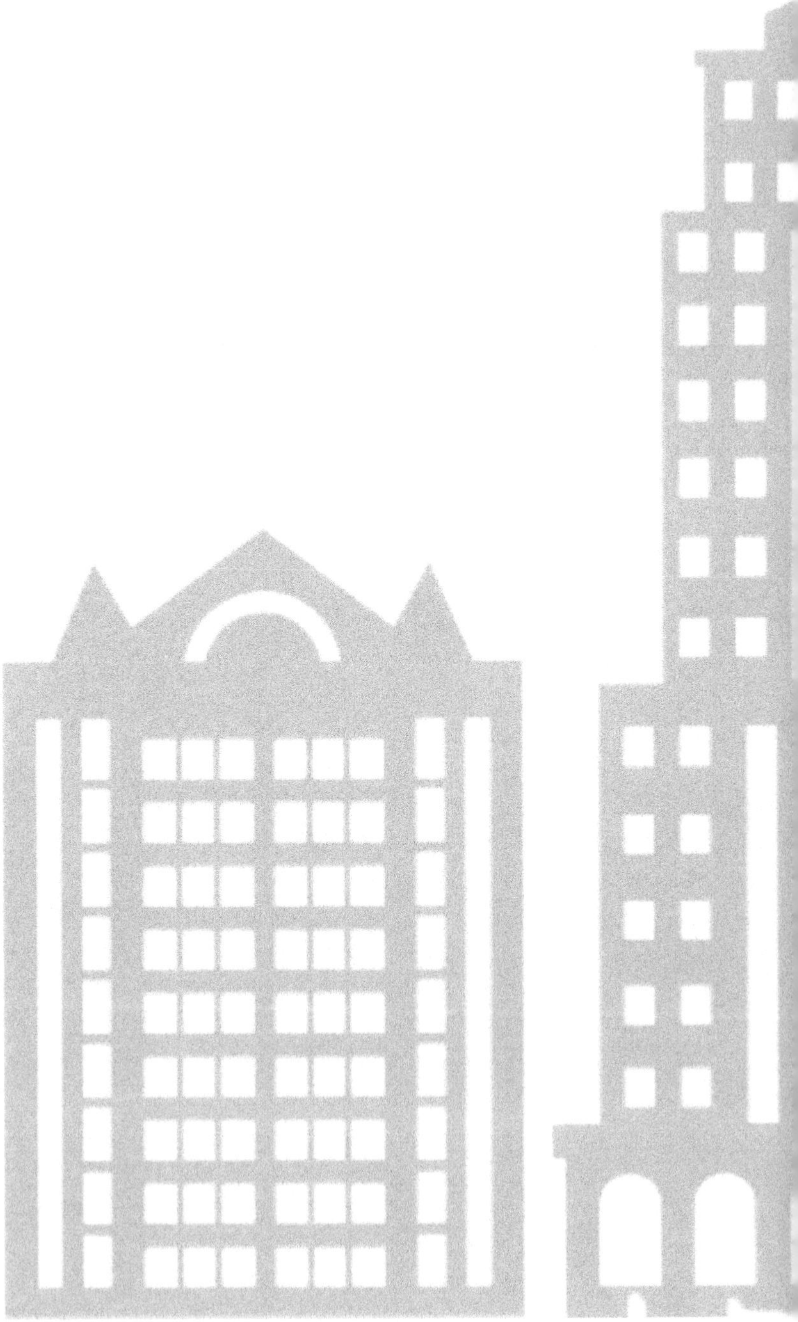

CHAPTER 4

The duo walked quickly across the lawn. Everyone waved and called good morning as they passed. Piper marveled at the community that Easton had established here.

"So, what faults does Easton have? Does he squash spiders in the most gruesome way ever?" Piper blurted. Then she felt her face heat when Sharon looked at her with an expression of complete confusion.

"Sorry! That came out of left field." Piper waved around the grounds. "It's just this seems too idyllic. How could one man create all this?"

Immediately, Sharon laughed. "Oh, Easton had some help. He's brilliant at finding the best people for a job and then leaving them alone to do what they do best. You'll find he's human and has his own faults. You'll discover them as he will deduce yours."

"You wouldn't want to clue me in and save me some time?" Piper suggested with a laugh as they stepped into the elevator.

"No way. You're on your own there."

Their friendship sealed, the women were still laughing when they reached Easton's office. Each must have looked guilty when they discovered their boss leaning against the admin's desk, waiting for them.

"No need to ask who you're laughing about," he said with a grin.

Piper sputtered, trying to figure out a way to not offend her new boss. "Come on, Little comedian. I'm hungry." Just as naturally as he accepted the two women's mirth, Easton took her hand and pulled her back into the elevator. Before Piper could process that her boss held her hand, he released it to press a button on the panel.

"Anything you avoid eating?" he asked casually.

To her horror, Piper burst into tears as Gabriel's correction after she'd eaten seafood lurched into her mind. She covered her face and cowered into the back corner while berating herself to get it together. *Be professional!*

A loud buzz made her look up in surprise. Easton moved from the elevator panel to settle against the wall before pulling his handkerchief from his jacket pocket. "Ah, Little girl. I'm so sorry I reminded you of something painful. I'd hug you, but I think you need to know you have the right to set boundaries for yourself."

She blinked at him. *Daddies get to make the rules, right? Little girls don't get to decide anything.*

"Here. Take this. Wipe your face and blow your nose. You are safe here. I've stopped the elevator to give us some time." Easton handed her the soft white cloth before he settled smoothly down on the floor. Braced against the wall, he gave her room but didn't withdraw from her. She was his focus. "Sit down. We'll wait until you're ready to tell me whatever I need to know."

"I'm sorry," she whispered as she awkwardly sat down in her slim skirt.

"We all have our garbage from crappy people in our lives. I'll never judge you for having a past or having feelings. I'm human, too."

"You never burst into tears over lunch," she guessed as she tried to get her feelings under control.

"I haven't. I don't usually let people get that close. One of my faults."

She stared at him in complete surprise. "You seem super friendly."

"Oh, I'm friendly. I genuinely like people and I love this company. Remembering that no one owes you anything in life has gotten me far. I reward those who are loyal," he shared. "Taking a personal risk is harder."

"Have you gotten hurt?" she blurted before thinking she shouldn't ask her new boss such sensitive questions.

Waving her hands in front of her, Piper signaled she wanted to erase that question. "Sorry."

"Tell me about him. Forget I'm your boss. I promise I won't hold anything against you. What did this pretend Daddy do?"

"Maybe he wasn't a pretend Daddy." Piper astonished herself by standing up for Gabriel.

"A real Daddy dom takes care of his Little, making her feel better about herself."

"I felt better about myself for a while. Then I found out he was using me to try to sneak in an underhanded deal with the company I worked for."

"I'm sorry he was a jerk."

Mouth falling open, Piper looked at Easton's concerned face. He was genuinely sorry that Gabriel had not treated her well. "I got my first spanking when I ate the seafood dish he had ordered for me rather than tell him I was allergic."

"That could have been serious. Were you okay?" Easton leaned forward.

"Some allergy medicine and topical anti-itch medicine and I was good," she rushed to reassure him.

"Good." He leaned back to rest his spine against the wall. "I'll offer suggestions, but let you choose your lunch."

"You're not my Daddy," she pointed out.

"Relationships take time, Little girl. We'll learn each other's quirks and talents to create a cohesive working team. If we're lucky, and I think the possibilities are high, we'll discover that we could be more for each other."

His last three words echoed in her mind. For each other. Gabriel had always been the one to determine what was going to happen. She'd thought he was taking care of her, but it turned out he was simply cultivating her job. "He sent me a text today."

"Can I see it?"

Nodding, Piper opened her phone and reread his words. She shivered at the threat. Scooting closer, Piper handed him her phone. She watched his face stiffen as he read.

"We'll show this to Knox before we leave for lunch. He's not finished. If his rationale for calling you his Little girl was simply to use you, this message doesn't make sense."

Easton paused to let that sink in for a minute. "What does make sense is we need to plan for the worst and be pleased when it doesn't happen. I can assure you that this man isn't a real Daddy. He wanted this message to scare you."

"Daddies don't scare their Littles?"

"No."

"They spank them," she insisted.

"They do when a spanking is effective. You may never trust a man to correct your behavior in this way again. For you, sitting in the corner, writing lines, even missing a fun event could be options that help you learn instead."

"Sounds like I'd be a lot of trouble as a Little. Probably not worth it."

"If you're a Little, that's in your DNA. You can't just switch off that part of you and pretend you're someone else. Well, you can, but eventually, you'll wake up and regret not living your true life."

He held his hand up to stop her when she opened her mouth to argue. "I'm not saying that you couldn't be happy—just that you'd know you missed out on something special."

Piper blew her nose to give herself time to think and then looked at him, horrified as she realized she'd just snotted all over his handkerchief. "I'm so sorry."

Easton's rich laughter was contagious. It did not bother him in the least. She couldn't help but giggle. As the laughter died out, everything crashed down on her. Trying to be brave, leaving all she knew to get away, having the man she thought was the love her life become her worst mistake, tears cascaded down her cheeks as she reached rock bottom.

"Oh, Little girl." Easton scooped her up easily in his arms and hugged her close.

Hiding her face against his crisp dress shirt, Piper clung to him.

His hands rubbed her back to console her. His muscles were relaxed underneath her, as if he was content to hold her as long as she needed him. Slowly, she felt the despair and unhappiness she'd pushed deep inside ease fractionally.

That small bit felt like the biggest step in finding herself once again. Piper felt her lips curve against his skin as she celebrated that gigantic step to surviving the blow that had rattled her so hard. Gabriel wouldn't win. Piper wouldn't let him mess with her head ever again.

"Seeing the light at the end of the tunnel?" he guessed.

"Y-yes," she breathed out in a shaky exhale. Then, realizing she sat on his lap, Piper scrambled away. She might have imagined it, but his arms seemed to tighten around her before he relaxed.

Easton took the handkerchief from her hand and found a clean corner. "Here, let me." He gently wiped away the trails of her tears from her cheeks and wiped the smudged mascara from her eyes. "There! If you smile, no one will know you were upset."

The intercom clicked on with a hum. "All okay, boss?" Knox's deep voice inquired softly.

"Thank you, Knox. We've finished our private conference and we're on the way down. Could you meet us at my entrance? I want you to read a message that came through on Piper's phone."

Piper's initial embarrassment in being caught with her boss doing heaven knows what in the private elevator on her first full day eased as Easton switched the focus to being proactive against Gabriel's threat. She grabbed the railing of the elevator and steadied herself as she stood. Reaching a hand down to Easton, she celebrated inside as he took her hand to let her tug him to his feet. She knew she didn't really help as he smoothly rose, but Piper liked the feeling that he'd accepted her assistance.

Easton released the hold on the elevator and sent it on its way down. They settled against intersecting walls—closer than they had been on the interrupted trip. Piper knew she should be embarrassed, but she wasn't. She felt comfortable with Easton. He'd already seen her worst and she looked forward to showing him her administrative skills.

In her head, she vowed, "I will be the best assistant Easton has ever had—even better than Sharon, with time!"

After stopping at the security desk to show the message to Knox, Easton escorted Piper across the campus to a gorgeous restaurant at the top of C building. It was packed with chattering employees. Everyone smiled or waved at Easton as they walked through the tables. Piper loved the friendly vibe that filled the room.

CHAPTER 5

Sitting back against the soft leather of the comfortable booth seat, Piper scanned the menu. She didn't know what to choose. Everything looked wonderful and expensive.

"Want a suggestion?" Easton asked as she looked back and forth, trying to decide.

"Yes!"

"Have the special with me."

"Did the server tell us what it was?"

"The chef's a friend of mine. He'll make something special just for us. I guarantee it will be delicious and we can request no seafood," he assured her.

She'd never done anything like that before. "Let's do it," Piper agreed, closing her menu with a snap.

Immediately, the server arrived to take their orders. She smiled as Easton ordered for the duo, alerting her to avoid seafood. "He's going to have fun today. A new seasonal produce item came in today for the first time. The chef is dying to experiment."

"Perfect!" Easton clapped his hands together in delight. When the server left to tell the chef the good news, he picked up his water glass and toasted Piper, "Here's to trying new things!"

"To new things!"

"After lunch, I'd like for us to look at the schedule and review my upcoming meetings."

"I'd like that. If it's okay, I'll ask some questions so I can get a feel for how you like to handle things. It looked like you always start out with a morning conference?" Piper re-created the schedule in her mind.

"That has been my normal procedure. Edgewater Industries is expanding to the point that I think these meetings are less effective. I'm only hearing from the top guy and while I ask for the complete picture, good and bad, there's some competition between the branches."

"Do you want my opinion?" she asked tentatively.

"Yes."

Piper smiled at his one-word answer. Easton didn't waste time on frilly pleasantries if something simpler could suffice. "How would you feel about a meeting with different positions in the various departments? For example, Sharon said there's a lot of concern about a new software program going in next month for the admins. Perhaps you could meet with random employees like me and the actual technology people ahead of the implementation and after, to answer questions or concerns."

"I like the idea of random employees. That takes it out of the hands of the managers. I bet tech could create a selection of people in different positions." Easton pulled out his phone to make notes.

"It's an interruption in people's day. That could be a negative for the highly dedicated employees you really want to hear from unless you tap into everyone's natural love of being recognized. Perhaps an Edgewater water bottle or some other small gift as a thank you?" Piper suggested hesitantly.

"I won't have room for each department every month. Maybe a rotation of two departments each month and one totally random employee draw?" Easton asked.

"I like that. I'd include everyone from the cafeteria workers to the top echelon of management." Piper watched her boss take notes. He really listened to her suggestions.

The server interrupted them as she brought their drinks. Easton hadn't ordered a cocktail but a simple unsweetened iced tea that Piper had echoed but switched to sweet. She took a big drink and wrinkled her nose at the bitter flavor. Glancing up at Easton, she laughed delightedly as he winced at the sugar.

"I'll signal her to bring a new glass for each of us," Piper suggested.

Easton held out his glass to her. "I don't have anything contagious. Do you?"

Piper felt her smile melt. She hadn't even thought of that. Gabriel had brought such havoc into her life. Could she trust he hadn't given her something as well?

"I'm sorry, Little girl. I should have thought before I spoke."

Waving a hand in the air, he flagged down their server. "Miss, could you bring us fresh drinks? I'm afraid you got our orders swapped. Sweet tea for the lady and regular for me, please."

With genuine apologies, she set off immediately to rectify the situation as Piper studied the tabletop intently. She didn't even know how to change the subject when her mind was tumbling through the what-ifs that besieged her. Piper missed seeing Easton send a quick message on his phone.

"You have an appointment at two this afternoon."

"What?" Surprised, Piper looked up to meet his gaze. She noted lines etched on his forehead.

"Every employee of Edgewater Industries has full benefits that begin on their first day of work. You have an appointment at the health center with our nurse practitioner at two. That's in the C tower. She will run all the tests you decide together should be checked."

"I can't ask you to do that," she protested, feeling her face heat at the same time she felt relief.

"You didn't ask. I arranged some care for my new assistant."

The arrival of the server with color-coded straws this time prevented any mix-up. "White for sugar. Red for warning, no sugar!"

Her cheerful joke broke the tension. When she left to check on their food, Piper said, "Thank you, Easton. I'll work late tonight to make up the time I miss."

"I'm going to send you home with an assignment," he warned. "You can work on it in your apartment before bed."

"Here you are! The chef hopes you'll love this. He's instructed me to tell you that this is your first course—a caprese salad." The server placed two beautiful plates before them. Fresh tomatoes glistened with a light sheen of oil on top of slices of fresh mozzarella. Thin shreds of basil decorated the top.

Piper forked a small bite into her mouth and groaned with delight. "Oh, yum!"

"Oh, yum, indeed," Easton echoed.

The pair sat quietly for several minutes as they enjoyed the simple but amazing dish. The flavor of each ingredient blended well. Even she could tell the chef had used the best ingredients, from the extra virgin olive oil to the freshly made cheese.

Finally, Piper laid her fork across her empty plate and sighed. "It was so good. I wonder what was seasonal? The tomatoes?"

"I bet we'll see for the next course," Easton suggested, nodding at the server who approached with two larger plates in her hands.

"Looks like the first course was a success," she complimented as she efficiently swapped the empty dishes for the new ones. "This is the main course—butter basil steak with roasted potatoes."

Piper leaned in to sniff the delicious aroma as she calculated the money left on her credit card to pay for this meal. She hadn't eaten a fancy steak at a restaurant in forever. Quickly, she forked a potato into her mouth and decided to enjoy the heck out of this meal.

Seeing her squirms of delight as she chewed, Easton suggested, "Wait until you try the steak." He lifted another piece of the thick filet to his mouth.

Quickly, she followed suit and popped a bite into her mouth. "Goodness. I think this is the best meal I've ever eaten."

"Now you know why I give the chef full power to create anything he wants."

"It can't always be this good," she marveled. "So, what's the magic ingredient he'd been waiting to try?"

"I believe it is basil."

"It's delicious!"

They each ate another bite, allowing the conversation to lapse as they enjoyed the food prepared especially for them. Soon, Easton began to ask her general questions, as if he truly wanted to get to know her better. The combination of good food, service, and a congenial lunch companion helped Piper relax. She realized she appreciated Easton more with each moment she spent with him.

"Ready for dessert?" the perky server asked as she brought more color-coded tea.

"I don't know that I can eat any more," Piper confessed.

"This is light. Trust me, you don't want to miss it."

"Bring it on," Easton encouraged.

She was back in a flash with two small golden bowls, each containing a single creamy white ball. "You are going to love this. Cinnamon basil ice cream."

"Basil ice cream?" Piper asked incredulously.

"Let's try it together. On the count of three. One. Two. Three." They each placed a small bite into their mouths and simultaneously groaned as the crisp, clean taste of cream, sugar, and a hint of cinnamon spice mixed with something exotic exploded.

"That is incredible," Piper commented as she scooped up another taste. As it melted in her mouth, she decided nothing could be better than the unique flavor. She froze as an image popped into her mind; Easton stretched out in a tub of milky liquid. His head propped against his forearm, the handsome silver fox watched her with an expression of tenderness and sexual tension. A sudden desire to taste his skin to see if he possibly could top this incredible flavor blossomed in her mind and she looked down to hide the heat she suspected must show in her eyes.

A warm hand covered hers as it pressed into the tabletop. Startled, Piper looked up into Easton's eyes. Instantly, she recognized the desire she'd concealed blazing hot in his gaze. *He feels the same way!*

"Take a breath, Piper."

Only then did the air rush back into her lungs as she realized she held her breath. His fingers curled between hers to squeeze her hand slightly. Before she could stop herself, Piper whispered, "Is this trouble?"

"Only the best kind."

CHAPTER 6

Piper sat on the paper-lined exam table, nervously waiting for the nurse practitioner. To give herself something to focus on other than sitting in a soft cotton gown with nothing else, she replayed the end of that exquisite meal. Easton had sent her on to the health center after the chef had come out to check on how they'd enjoyed lunch. She'd protested not paying for her meal, but the chef had put an end to that.

"No charge for guests of Mr. Edgewater. I appreciate you being my guinea pig."

"It was delicious," she'd complimented as she slid from the booth. "Thank you, Easton."

Upon reaching the door, Piper had realized the health center hadn't been on Sharon's tour and she did not know where to go. Her phone had buzzed, drawing her attention. Opening a message, she'd felt her lips curve in a delighted grin as a map of the grounds appeared on her phone.

The opening of the door drew her from her thoughts. A kind-looking woman in her late forties stepped into the room with a crisp folder. "Ms. Townie?"

"Yes, I'm Piper."

"I'm Sarah Trimble, the nurse practitioner for the health center. Congratulations on your new job. What brought you in today?"

Words tumbled from Piper's mouth. "I just fled a menacing relationship…"

The nurse probed when Piper paused, uncertain of what to ask for. "An intimate relationship?"

"Yes."

"Then we'll test any health concerns for everything and give you some peace of mind. Before we start, do you have health concerns that I need to know about?"

"No. I'm pretty healthy. I haven't been sleeping well, though," she confessed.

"Sleep is important. I'll see if I can come up with some suggestions for you to try. Let me do a quick check before we take some samples for the lab." With calm assurance, the nurse examined her.

Fifteen minutes later, a bevy of tubes and capped swabs sat on the tray, ready to go to the lab. She had sent a new prescription for birth control to the pharmacy. "Okay, Piper. I'll send you a message when I get the test results back. Use condoms until we get all the results back. You're very healthy. I have a feeling that the sleep trouble stems from what you've been through lately. Starting a new job alone can be stressful. Combine that with everything else and it's no wonder you have trouble sleeping."

"My stress level has been sky high," Piper admitted.

"Let's work on helping you relax before turning out the lights. Set a usual time for bed and stick to that. I'll recommend nine p.m. No electronics, work, or exercise an hour before bed. Consider adding a drop of lavender essential oil to your pillow or rub it on your nightshirt. Take a warm bath or have a warm, non-caffeinated drink before bed. The traditional warm milk works perfectly and is good nutritionally as well."

Piper nodded. "I'll try it. Thank you."

"I'm glad to meet you, Piper. Come see me regularly. I want you healthy and happy here. If you're not aware of your benefits here at Edgewater Industries, all medical, dental, and mental health treatments are covered completely. That includes your prescriptions and over-the-counter medicine. Visit the pharmacy to pick up anything that you need."

"Thank you, Sarah. I'm glad to meet you, too. This could have been very embarrassing. You made it okay."

"Then I did my job." Sarah patted her on the knee and picked up the tray and folder. "Get some sleep."

After watching the door close behind the comforting figure, Piper wrapped her arms around herself in a tight hug. That certainly hadn't been fun, but it hadn't been awful either. And best of all, it was done. All except the waiting.

Glancing at the clock in the room, Piper knew she'd have time to get back to the office before the close of the day. The efficient nurse had completed all the tests and different parts of the exam in a short amount of time. Piper hopped up from the table and started dressing.

The whisper sound of a desk drawer opening and closing reached Easton as he studied the latest financial reports. He felt his lips curve. It made him happy to have Piper close. She'd made an impact on him in a brief time. Sharon was a very sharp woman to have selected her for him to interview.

She worked quietly at her desk in the outer room. Easton had marked himself out of the office on the computer system so that he could focus on decoding the numbers contained in the report. Something was off. It was subtle, but he always paid attention to his intuition.

"Piper?" Easton called into the intercom.

When she appeared in his doorway, he smiled at her. "Thanks for coming back to work. Turns out I need your help. Could you contact Barry Mattson in accounting? If he's in the building, would you ask him to come talk to me?"

"Of course." Piper turned and accessed the number he'd given her that morning. Thank goodness for Sharon!

"Barry, this is Piper in Mr. Edgewater's office. He asked me to call to see if you're still at your desk?"

She was quiet for a few seconds while he obviously answered. "Perfect. Could you come to his office?"

Piper looked concerned as she disconnected the call. "Barry is on his way. He told me to let you know he's bringing his computer, and the most recent updates are in your inbox now."

"Thank you, Piper. This meeting will take a while." He looked up at the clock. "I don't want you to wait until we finish hashing out this report. I left a few things on your desk. Would you wait to show Barry into my office and then you can take off for the evening?"

"I'd like to work here for a while if you don't mind. I'm getting the knack of Sharon's organization, but need to explore a bit."

"Of course, Piper. Whatever helps you settle in comfortably here. No working after you leave the office then. Those tasks I left can wait until another day. I want you out of here by seven at the latest."

"I hope you aren't here too late, sir."

He smiled at the title she gave him. "I'm used to late nights, but thank you."

A noise in the outer office made her straighten up from leaning on the door frame. "Barry is here. I'll show him in."

"Thank you, Piper. Close the door behind him, please."

In seconds, Barry entered with his computer in hand and a set of printouts. "Hi, Easton. Thanks for pulling me in. I sent you an email about an hour ago, but hadn't gotten a response. My plan was to call for an appointment tomorrow morning. I should have known this would ding on your radar as well."

"Sit down, Barry. Let's figure this out," Easton invited as the door closed quietly behind the accountant.

"Yours?" Barry asked, glancing at the closed door.

"She's mine."

"Congratulations."

"About damn time I found her."

Easton felt his lips curl in a smile as the other man pulled a chair close to his desk to arrange his computer and documents. "Let's dive in. Let me show you what I found."

Two hours later, Easton had all the proof he needed. He called Knox to come to his office. When Piper let the security chief in, he looked at her sternly. "Go back to your apartment, Piper."

"On my way. Can I get you all a cup of coffee before I leave or order something for dinner?"

"We're almost done here, Piper. We'll follow you out in a few minutes."

"I'll see you in the morning."

"Sleep well," he encouraged.

"Thank you. Goodnight, gentlemen."

"Goodnight, Piper," Barry said, closely echoed by Knox.

When the door closed again, Knox met Easton's gaze. "I'm glad you listened to Sharon."

"I am, too."

CHAPTER 7

When Piper arrived the next morning, Sharon sat at her desk—this time on the opposite side. "Good morning! I can sit over there," Piper assured Sharon.

"You might as well get used to that chair," Sharon answered with a serene smile.

When she saw Piper glance at Easton's closed door, she added, "He's in a meeting with the legal department. You'll see, even in a company as supportive of employees like Edgewater Industries, there are bad people. As the admin, you'll see some of them. Knox met two people at the gate today with their personal items. He confiscated their ID badges and computers. They were not allowed back on the grounds."

Piper nodded and understood just how serious the conversation between the three men had been last night. *Who would risk a job here?* Shaking her head in disbelief, she started to mention last night's events to Sharon but decided to stay quiet.

"I'll grab a cup of coffee and we'll get started. I left a list of questions to ask you."

"Bring them on!" Sharon laughed.

"Can I bring you a cup?" Piper asked, putting a pod into the automatic brewer and pressing the button.

"No, thanks. I just made this one."

Piper brought her cup back to the desk and sat awkwardly in the chair. She felt strange using it when Sharon had sat there for so many years. To distract herself, Piper pulled the pad of paper in front of her and flipped to a page of notes that she had made after Sharon left.

The two women were almost through the list when the door to Easton's office opened. "Good morning, ladies. I see you're hard at work already. I had a late night and need an infusion of coffee."

"I can bring it to you," Piper offered, standing.

Easton waved her back into her seat. "Don't let me interrupt you. I can push a button with the best of them. When Knox appears, please send him in."

"Yes, sir," Piper answered with a nod.

"You can call me Easton for now," he said gently with a smile.

Piper looked down at the papers in neat stacks on the desk and subtly blinked the tears from her eyes. She pretended to read one of the printed sheets. *Stop it!* She didn't want to be unprofessional in the office.

Efficiently, Easton brewed his coffee and walked back to his office. At the doorway, he asked quietly, "Piper, if you have a moment, I'd like to talk to you."

Trying to compose her face, Piper stood and walked to the door. "Yes, Easton. What can I do for you?"

"Close the door."

Swallowing hard, she repeated over and over in her mind, "Get it together. Get it together," as she quietly followed his directions.

"Piper, I apologize. I didn't mean to upset you."

She looked up at him in shock. *How does he know?*

"Someday, perhaps, you'll be ready to move on from your ordeal. I will never rush you or force a relationship that you don't wish. I do want you to know that when you're ready, I'm waiting."

"He shattered me," Piper choked out.

"He tried to shatter you, but you're resilient. You left. You didn't stay in a dangerous situation, and you came here where you're safe."

She stared at him. "I don't know if I can recover."

"That's crap. You're already recovering. Each day you're stronger."

He opened a drawer to flick out a couple of tissues. Approaching, he lifted one to her face and hesitated, asking permission. After a brief pause, she nodded, and Easton gently blotted the moisture from the corners of her eyes. Automatically, she lowered her eyelids.

His warmth radiated toward her. When she felt his lips press a soft kiss to her forehead, she took one step closer to press herself against his heat. Easton's arms wrapped around her to hold her tight. He didn't say anything but was simply content to comfort her.

She relaxed against his chest, dropping her cheek to rest on his crisp dress shirt. Her eyes closed as he stroked a slow hand up and down her spine. Time seemed to freeze around them as Piper memorized the feel of Easton holding her. His masculine, clean scent filled her nostrils. Piper had never dated a man with a beard. Easton's short salt-and-pepper scruff looked bristly, but she was delighted with the silky feel of his hair against her skin.

Even his beard takes care of me. A quick giggle escaped her lips at this thought.

"It makes me happy to hold you, too," he said softly.

The rumble of Knox's voice in the outer office made her step back from his embrace. She smiled tentatively at him and received a slow wink in response. A light feeling gathered inside her, seeming to push away the darkness that had loomed over Piper since she'd fled from Gabriel.

"Go let Knox in, Little girl. Remember, you're safe here in every way."

Nodding, she turned and walked to the door. Piper hesitated and looked over her shoulder at him. "Thanks, Easton."

"I'm always here for you."

As lunch approached, Sharon explained the last thing on Piper's list to go over. A rapid banging sound on the door down the hall made both women look up. At the sound of "Mommy," Sharon stood up quickly and walked into the passageway.

"Roger? Hi, Little boy. Did you come to find me?" Sharon asked, guiding a large man into the office.

"Mommy! I was lost. I remembered you worked on the top floor, but I couldn't find you."

"You were supposed to stay in our apartment, Roger," she gently reminded him.

"I couldn't do that. You were lost!" He looked at her in confusion.

Piper realized that this must be Sharon's husband. He was tall and muscular but stooped with rounded shoulders. His hands flailed by his sides, revealing his agitation. His face contorted in a look of frustration. It looked as if somewhere in his mind, Roger knew he wasn't making sense with both him and Sharon being lost separately. To distract him, Piper stood and walked forward to greet him.

"You must be Roger. I'm Piper."

Roger looked at her blankly before slowly lifting his hand to shake hers. His body operated on instinct from years of interacting appropriately with others. His face relaxed as she took his hand to shake it. This was familiar and routine.

"I came to get Mommy. She needs to come home now," he told Piper.

"Okay. I bet she's ready to spend time with you."

"Let me grab my purse, Roger, and we'll be off." Sharon met Piper's eyes, sending her a silent apology that she couldn't finish the topic they'd been discussing.

Piper shook her head slightly and smiled. "Have a wonderful afternoon, you two. I'll see how many questions I can come up with for tomorrow," she joked.

"Can we have ham… ham…, you know, those things with potato sticks?" Roger stumbled over the words as if they eluded him.

"We had hamburgers and fries last night for dinner. How about something more nutritious?" Sharon asked.

"No, Mommy. Ham and sticks."

"You got it, Roger. We'll grab a couple of burgers." She wrapped an arm around his waist and guided him to the door. Sharon pasted a smile on her face as she looked up at him.

Piper's heart hurt for her new friend at the sadness reflected in

Sharon's eyes. Sending her a wave of mental support, Piper stood in the office watching Sharon guide a stumbling, uncoordinated Roger through the door. His voice drifted back to Piper as Roger repeated his request for the fast-food treat. Their voices died out when they stepped into the elevator.

"Roger was the local bank president. He left his job when the doctors diagnosed him with rapid onset dementia. It's hard for everyone to see his decline—heartbreaking for his Little girl who now has become his Mommy. Sharon refuses to hire a caregiver for Roger until there is no other option," Easton shared quietly.

"She loves him very much," Piper observed.

"He has been her life for twenty years." Easton rubbed the back of his neck and confessed, "I didn't know if she'd be able to come in for the entire week of training that we promised you. My guess is she'll want to answer questions on the phone from now on."

"That would be okay. I know where everything is now. Well, almost!" Piper said with a laugh.

"We keep our electronic records filed precisely. Sharon usually disperses my email into the correct place to free me up for other work. Would you mind taking care of this after lunch?"

"Yes. Sharon demonstrated this with her mailbox. I'll file everything I know where it goes and check with Sharon on anything that doesn't make sense."

"Thank you, Piper."

CHAPTER 8

Sitting in her quiet apartment, Piper finally had time to really think. She remembered the feel of Easton's arms around her and hugged herself tightly. He felt—right. Being in his arms evoked a range of emotions, from comfort to desire to fear.

"Not everyone is a using jerk who plays on your fantasies!" Piper rebuked herself aloud.

The apartment was suddenly too quiet. Piper hadn't seen anyone in the lobby as she'd entered the building. Maybe she should go knock on Regina's door and see if she'd like to hang out for a while. Standing, she walked to the big window and looked out. There were still a lot of people milling around the grounds. Piper considered going outside to enjoy the evening air but didn't want to sit there all alone.

Her gaze lifted to study the building across from her. Piper glanced up at the top floor to see if her office faced her apartment. She leaned closer to the glass. Easton stood against the railing of the balcony on the top floor. Shirtless, he held a water bottle in his hand, drinking from it.

Damn! She memorized his toned body from afar, wishing she could see him better. Piper had suspected that he worked hard to stay in shape. Even from this distance, she could confirm that.

Slowly turning his head, Easton seemed to scan the area. When his gaze landed on her window, he raised a hand to say, "Hi."

Automatically, she stepped away from the glass, feeling self-conscious. She jumped when her phone buzzed in her pocket. Looking at the screen, she read his message.

Popcorn and an action movie are next on my plans. Want to join me?

As if working by themselves, Piper's fingers typed out a reply: *I'd love to.*

Not allowing herself to second guess her response, Piper dashed to her bedroom and pulled on her sneakers. Brushing her hair, she looked down at the shorts and t-shirt she wore. Was this okay to go spend time with her boss?

Who am I kidding? Nothing's appropriate to wear to spend time with your boss.

Pushing all the negative thoughts from her mind, Piper grabbed her phone and keys. She almost turned back when she had to wait for the elevator, but Piper drove those worries from her mind. Easton drew her to him. She wanted to be with him more than she was afraid to screw things up.

Dashing across the beautiful lawn, she took the private elevator up to the office. When the doors opened, she stepped into the office. Easton walked through his office door, pulling on a T-shirt. His hair was wet and tousled. Heat built low in her stomach as she pictured him naked in the shower.

He reached out a hand for hers. "Come on. My apartment's this way." He gently tugged her through his office, private bathroom, and into a large open space. The panoramic windows reveal a magnificent view of Edgewater Industries.

"No wonder you were out on the balcony," she commented, taking another step forward without watching where she was going. With a thump, she ran into his side.

With concern written on his face, Easton wrapped an arm around Piper to steady her. Turning, he drew her closer, holding Piper against his body. Her heart rate jumped as she stared up into his handsome face. Unable to resist the desire brewing inside her, Piper rose onto her toes to glide her hands around the back of his neck. She didn't know who moved first, but their mouths pressed together softly.

A sound of delight escaped her as she pulled his head down again to taste him more deliberately. His flavor eased through her mouth as Easton took control of the kiss and licked the crease of her lips, silently asking for her to open her mouth. When she willingly invited him in, Easton swept his tongue through the inside of her mouth. He moved slowly and deliberately, teasing her tongue with his and tempting her to respond.

Piper wiggled closer, enjoying being the center of his attention. Thrilling her, she felt him hardening against her. Easton slid a hand down her spine and over the curve of her bottom. His fingers tightened slightly on her rounded flesh to pull her in, erasing the millimeter of distance between their bodies.

"Little girl, what you do to me," he growled against her lips. This time, his mouth captured hers hard. He cupped the back of her head with his other hand and held her steady as he explored her.

Ripping his mouth away to allow them both to gasp for oxygen, Easton searched her face before asking, "Movie or my bed, Piper?"

Piper closed her eyes to hide for a moment from his knowing gaze. She could only think of touching him. Forcing herself to ask the question lurking in her mind, she whispered, "I want you so bad, but I don't want to make another mistake. I don't want you to think I'm the type that falls into bed with any man."

Easton pressed a kiss to her forehead, sending a shiver of delight through Piper at his response. Her eyelids flew open to allow her to scan his face. There were no signs of anger.

"Then we watch a movie and get to know each other better. When you know it's right for us to be together, you'll be ready. I've waited for you all my life. I can easily wait a bit longer."

He shook his head with a devilish grin. "That's a total lie. It's not going to be easy to wait. But Piper, when you go crazy in my arms, I'll demand all you can give me."

Nodding without thought, Piper stroked through his salt-and-pepper hair. She loved the banked heat in his eyes. Easton was in full control of himself. He wanted her. Rising to her toes, she kissed him again, trying to express her appreciation.

"Come on, Little girl. Let's get comfortable on the couch. I want you close to me," Easton told her softly when she lifted her lips. Guiding her to the curved leather sectional, he sat and tugged her into position, snuggled next to him.

After one more kiss, he turned on the large display. A debate over the movie to choose followed. They discovered they liked a lot of the same types of movies. With their selection made, Easton revealed his addiction to popcorn.

"I thought we'd just throw a bag in the microwave," Piper confessed when he opened the cabinet under the TV to reveal neatly stacked plastic containers of gourmet popcorn.

"My weakness, I'm afraid. What's your favorite: buttered, cheese, cinnamon, or caramel?"

"I like cheese and caramel mixed," she dared to share.

Easton pulled out the largest container and opened the seal to reveal beautiful orange and brown popcorn nestled inside. "I've been saving this for a special occasion. It's my absolute favorite."

He settled back down on the couch and tugged her close. Pressing a soft kiss to Piper's lips, Easton growled, "I knew you were perfect!"

Before she could protest, he flicked on the movie and lifted a kernel of popcorn to her lips. "Eat, Baby girl. I'm glad you're here."

The early morning sun streamed into the apartment, casting a beam of light over Piper's face. She shifted an arm to shield her eyes and felt her pillow move underneath her. Blinking open her eyes, she stared into Easton's mesmerizing green ones. "Hi!" she whispered.

"Good morning, Little girl." His voice was deep and gravelly, still filled with sleep. Just that sound kindled desire deep in her abdomen.

"We must have fallen asleep?" she guessed.

"That second movie proved to be the bedtime story for us." Easton's hand stroked her hair away from her face before tracing a line down her cheek and over her neck to cup her shoulder. "Kiss me good morning."

His tone was gentle but firm. She responded immediately, without hesitation. Pressing her lips to his in a soft butterfly kiss, she wiggled closer to deepen the connection. "Mmm!"

"Just the way I want to start my morning."

She got lost in his eyes. He looked at her as no one ever had. Aroused and caring, Piper felt like she was the center of his universe. She liked it—a lot. Feeling the corners of her lips curve in a contented smile, she basked in his attention.

Beep! Beep! An alarm sounded on his watch. Quickly, he silenced it with a tap.

"What time it is? I have to get back to my apartment." Already, the thought of a walk of shame from her boss' home back to her apartment made her face heat with embarrassment.

"Let's finish our jog," he said.

"What jog?"

"Our jog through the greenspace."

Totally confused, Piper watched him stand to grab her shoes from the end of the couch where he'd dropped them after insisting she make herself comfortable. Easton set them on the coffee table and lowered himself before her to cradle one of Piper's feet in his hand.

"I can do it," she said in confusion, reaching for one sneaker.

"My job," he answered, claiming the shoe and sliding it over her toes and into position. Easton tied it snug before repeating the action with the other shoe.

Rising athletically to his feet, he tugged her up from the couch. "Go potty and wash your face."

Confused, she followed his directions before rejoining him. With a warm hand on Piper's low back, Easton steered her to the elevator. When they emerged into the bright sunlight, he took her hand and began a slow jog.

It took Piper a couple of steps to figure out he really meant they were going for a jog. When she was steady, he dropped her hand, and the two moved fluidly next to each other. Already, several early birds moved around the green areas. Some jogged just as they were.

Easton waved at the people they passed and shouted, "Good morning."

The first few times, Piper felt her face heat with embarrassment. Quickly, she figured out that Easton had engineered a perfect way for her to return to her apartment without attracting any attention. When they reached the building, she turned to thank him, but Easton waved her into the building ahead of him. He pressed his fingerprint against the pad to call the elevator and ushered her into the car.

"Take your time. I'll see you in the office." When she nodded, he stepped out and waited to see the doors close.

Daringly, she blew him a kiss. His answering wolfish smile thrilled her. Easton evoked feelings in her she'd never experienced. Comparing them to what she'd thought was so spectacular in her relationship with Gabriel made the other man's attentions seem narcissistic and selfish.

If I'd only known!

CHAPTER 9

Arriving even later than Piper, Sharon had rushed in, apologizing. "I'm sorry. Things were crazy at home this morning. Unfortunately, I'll need to leave in a couple of hours to take Roger to the doctor."

"Sharon, we could set up a time to talk on the phone each day now if I have questions. I know you're busy," Piper suggested.

The frazzled woman dropped into her chair with a relieved sigh. "That would be amazing. I'll come in if I can but if life is nuts, I'll send you a message. We can figure out when to schedule a call."

Piper stood and walked to the coffeepot. Making herself a cup, she brewed another as Sharon logged into the network. She carried the cup over to her friend.

"You're an angel," Sharon thanked her gratefully as she took the cup.

"No, but I'm happy you think so!" Piper chirped. "Here's my first question. I'm clearing out Easton's inbox and there are a bunch of emails marked P for private? I don't know what to do with them."

"P is the designation for personnel. It's also protected information, so you don't want to read it," Sharon clarified.

"Got it. Where is that stored electronically?"

"Open up the Human Relations folder on the shared drive. Each year, I start a file named E. Edgewater and the year. Open that and you'll see all the months. Just choose the right one and file away."

"Great system," Piper complimented, quickly filing the last emails away.

"It works for me. Feel free to adapt anything. It needs to be user friendly for you. Easton gets a ton of notifications. I've suggested he send them to someone else to be aware of any problems, but Easton wants to have his finger on the everyday stuff as well as the long-range plans of the company. I don't know how he has time for everything. He doesn't sleep."

"What? He has to sleep," Piper protested. Her mind automatically flashed back to waking cuddled up to him.

"He grabs a few hours of sleep each day. Easton looks more rested today than ever."

"Good. He needs to rest and recharge," Piper stated. If she could help him sleep more, maybe she would be as good for him as she thought he was for her.

"Sharon, good to see you. Piper, could I steal you away for a minute?" Easton stood in the doorway, looking devastatingly handsome in his crisp gray suit.

Piper grabbed her notebook and pen before standing to walk toward him. Trying to be subtle, her gaze devoured his appearance. The picture of him rumpled and a breath away flashed into her mind as she approached. To her dismay, Piper tripped slightly over the toe of one pump. Easton immediately stepped forward to catch her. His powerful hands on her arms steadied her.

"Whoa, Little girl. Don't scare me," he whispered for her ears only. His gaze captured hers and heat immediately flared between them.

"I'm so sorry. Thank you for keeping me from falling," she answered.

"I plan to always be there for you."

Raising his voice, he added, "I want to go over this afternoon's schedule with you."

Easton closed the door behind them before leaning close to press a soft kiss to her lips. "Good morning, again."

"Good morning," she whispered before being brave and rising on her toes to kiss him again.

"Temptress. Sit and let me walk you through what's on the schedule today."

Efficiently, he ran through the afternoon meetings on his schedule, laying out what he needed her to do. Piper appreciated his management style. She enjoyed knowing what his expectations were. Eventually, she would automatically understand how his administrative assistant could support his duties. For now, his training was every bit as valuable as Sharon's insights and guidance.

"Got it. I see you have dinner with the head of Riverbend Industries at seven. May I make reservations for you?" Piper asked with a smile as they finished up.

"I would appreciate that, Piper. See if L'Orangerie can squeeze me in for a table for two," he requested.

"I'll call as soon as they open," she promised, making herself a note.

"Thank you. No visitors this morning, Piper. I have a lot to organize in my brain."

"Got it." With a smile, she stood and walked to the door. "Let me know if you need anything."

"Will do," he answered, already distracted by a file on his screen.

Quietly, Piper let herself out of the office and returned to her desk. "Know who to talk to at L'Orangerie for a table tonight?" she asked Sharon.

"They snatch reservations up there a month in advance. The only person who might get you squeezed in is Knox," Sharon counseled.

"Knox? The head of security?" Piper asked in bewilderment.

"Yes. Knox has a wide net of contacts. Before Easton convinced him to work at Edgewater Industries, Knox worked in private security, coordinating personal guards for the most influential celebrities and businesspeople. He knows everyone. And even more important, everyone respects him."

Nodding, Piper selected his number and called.

"You okay, Piper? Any more messages?" Knox's gruff voice asked instantly.

ne. Thank you for being concerned. No more messages," she quickly. "I called to see if I could ask a favor."

"...urse. What can I do for you?"

"It's a long shot, but Mr. Edgewater would like to take an associate to L'Orangerie this evening. I know it's a lot to ask…"

"I'll make a call. What time?"

"Seven?"

"I'll do my best." Without a goodbye, he disconnected.

Piper smiled at Sharon, understanding the gruff man's abruptness. "He's on the job. There's a lot to Knox, isn't there?"

"Yes."

Sharon's gaze slid to her computer screen, and she changed the subject. "Let's talk computer safety."

After discussing all the built-in protection on the Edgewater servers, Sharon concluded with one last piece of advice. "If something seems weird, listen to your intuition. Contact Knox and Belinda."

"Will do."

"I'm out of here. We'll touch base tomorrow about setting up a call when you have more questions."

"Thanks, Sharon."

Piper watched Sharon bustle from the room. Her heart went out to the other woman. Her stress level was palpable. Losing her husband one bit at a time had to be gut-wrenching. Stepping away from a job she'd had for years, Piper knew had to destroy Sharon's equilibrium alone. She vowed to help the woman who'd become a close friend so quickly.

Managing the bustling office, Piper buried herself in the tasks she needed to complete before the meetings. Several staff members messaged for meetings with Easton throughout the morning. She skillfully found places in her boss' schedule.

When her growling stomach interrupted her, Piper glanced up to see that Easton's first meeting would start in forty-five minutes. "Had he even eaten breakfast?" she wondered.

Piper decided to knock on his door to see if she could get him some lunch. Two steps away, her phone buzzed. Looking at the screen, Piper's heart melted just a bit more.

"Come in and lock the door behind you. I have sandwiches ready in my apartment."

Stepping through the door, she twisted the lock and headed through the interior door. An appetite-inducing aroma met her as she stepped into his familiar home. "Wow! That smells amazing."

"Security just brought them up the back way. Still hot from the deli," he tempted her. "I ordered a whole sandwich. Half is yours."

"I don't want to steal your lunch," she protested.

"There's no way I can eat a whole sub from DiMarco's. Come sit." Easton pulled out a chair at his counter and helped her into place.

"No seafood," he promised, unwrapping the waxed paper.

"I was just coming to see if I could pick up a sandwich for you in the cafeteria," she laughed as he placed a huge half a sub on the plate in front of her. "I can't eat all that. A half is like a meal for three."

"Eat what you like," Easton suggested as he lifted his glass of tea to toast her.

Expecting that he had forgotten she liked sweet tea, Piper took a tentative taste. "Mmm! That's wonderful. Don't tell me I've tempted you to the sweet side."

"You have tempted me to the sweet side, but I'll stick with my regular tea," he answered with a smile.

There was no mistaking the message in those words. Piper felt her heart flutter inside her chest. "Thank you."

"I enjoy taking care of you. Eat. Tell me what you think of our local deli."

Piper felt like she needed to unhinge her jaw to take a bite. They'd piled everything in between toasted pieces of delicious Italian bread. She moaned in delight at the savory meat and all the toppings.

"Good, isn't it?" Easton asked before taking an enormous bite himself. A dollop of spicy mustard dropped from the sandwich to land on his shirt.

"Good thing you live here. You can grab a fresh shirt," she teased as he tried to dab at the stain and only made it worse.

"You don't have any clothes here yet. Here. Let's put this around you," Easton instructed, grabbing a large cloth napkin and draping it around her neck. He tucked the ends into her dress' neckline behind her head. "Voila! Protected."

"Thanks." Piper smoothed the napkin over her chest before taking another bite.

They ate, interspersing conversation with periods of comfortable quiet. Piper felt herself relax as she had last night. Being with Easton made her happy. Finally, she had to wrap up half of her sandwich. She couldn't eat another bite. Piper smiled as she watched Easton pop the last bite of his into his mouth.

"Want to eat the rest of mine?" she asked.

"No way. I'd fall into a carb coma halfway through the meeting. Stick it in the fridge," he suggested as he stood. As she moved through the kitchen, Easton pulled off his tie and unbuttoned the stained shirt.

Piper turned around and froze. She'd seen Easton shirtless before but was amazed by his chiseled form each time she had the opportunity to study him. Easton looked incredible in a dress shirt and suit jacket, but without them, he was jaw-droppingly magnetic.

Gabriel had been solid strength. His lean form had amazed Piper and turned her on. That bastard couldn't compare to Easton's body, rippled with mature musculature attesting to a lifetime of fitness. Her fingers ached to trace the pathways down his abs, following that silvery-black wispy trail of hair.

"Little girl." His deep tone demanded her compliance. "Eyes on mine."

Her gaze reluctantly lifted to meet his. Desire radiated from his green eyes, pushing her arousal higher. Piper clenched her thighs together, trying to control the wetness that dampened her panties.

"I can't go into the meeting with an erection. Nor do we have time to satisfy our hunger now," he growled, holding a hand up to stop her step toward him. "After, you're mine."

Daringly, Piper allowed her gaze to trace down his torso once again. His cock pressed thickly against the straining zipper of his dress slacks. There was no mistaking that Easton was gifted in other areas besides business skills. Her unintentional lick of her lips evoked a somewhat pained sound from deep inside him.

"Go now, Little girl."

She turned and fled from his apartment. Closing the door behind her, Piper leaned against it. She blew out her breath and tried to convince her heart to stop beating so fast.

You're in the office. Get yourself under control.

Even after talking sternly to herself, all she wanted to do was go back inside. Peeling herself from the hardwood panel, Piper gave herself a shake and forcibly switched herself into efficient administrative assistant mode. She straightened her skirt and walked from Easton's office.

Fifteen minutes until the first attendee arrived. Piper double-checked that she'd set the conference table with all the materials Easton had requested. Realizing that she'd forgotten to set pens on the table, Piper quickly found a new box in the supply cabinet. Squeaking wheels alerted her that the refreshments from the cafeteria arrived. The hustle and bustle of the last-minute details distracted her from replaying the sight of Easton in her mind.

"Daryl! I'm glad you made it," Easton greeted the arriving guest as he stepped from his office. He shook the arriving businessman's hand.

The other meeting attendees arrived in clusters. Piper and Easton worked efficiently with each other to get everyone settled into a place at the table. Piper sat slightly behind Easton, out of the line of vision of everyone, but close enough to take notes.

"Ladies and gentlemen, thank you for joining me here today. If you haven't met my new administrative assistant, this is Piper." Easton swept a hand her way as he turned toward Piper.

Only visible to her, his slow wink made her miss the first few sentences as he began the meeting.

CHAPTER 10

Piper sat on the couch in her apartment, trying to not be jealous of the company president Easton had taken to dinner after the long meeting. Dressed in the oversized T-shirt she wore to bed, Piper described the day to Stanley, her best friend in the entire world. The teddy bear sat absorbing all the details she shared with a sympathetic look on his face.

"Stanley, I thought he was going to ravish me on the kitchen table, but now he's out to dinner with Ava Scalon. She was very nice, but I kinda hate her right now."

The bear's eyes darkened a bit and Piper knew exactly what he was thinking. "I know it's not right to hate anyone. But I want to be with him now." Piper flounced back against the pillows and crossed her arms over her chest.

When the well-loved bear didn't answer, Piper looked out the side of her eye to read his expression. Frowning, she admitted, "I know that's not fair. She didn't do anything wrong. Easton had already decided to take the company president out to dinner before our explosive lunch together."

Unable to resist, Piper used her phone to pull up the menu at L'Orangerie. Written in French with English descriptions and no prices. Piper had never eaten anywhere fancy. Looking at the website, she decided the French restaurant might be a tad intimidating. One picture featured the elegantly set table. Shining silverware bracketed the plate, and Piper counted three forks alone. *What do you eat with each of those?* Maybe it was a good thing Ava Scalon was there instead of her.

As a lark, she created a menu selection for herself and one for Stanley. "You can have escargots, boeuf bourguignon, and crème brûlée. I think I'll have soupe a l'oignon gratinee, saumon, and tarte aux fruits," she announced in a fake French accent that wouldn't have been recognizable in any French-speaking country.

Joining Stanley in his giggles, Piper dropped her phone to the couch and fell back against the cushions. The stress of the day slipped away as she enjoyed the company of her oldest friend.

"Thanks, Stanley," she whispered. "I needed that."

She scooped the well-loved teddy bear up and hugged him tightly. Sitting quietly for a few moments, Piper tried to understand the feelings whirling around inside her. She'd promised herself to stay away from men and had decided never to trust a Daddy again. Easton wasn't allowing her to stick to that plan.

"I guess I was so wrapped up in the fantasy of having a Daddy that I fell for the first one that found me. That wasn't my most logical move, Stanley. I should have known better," she told her friend confidentially.

"What do I do about Easton?"

Piper searched her stuffie's expression. Stanley seemed to be listening intently. *Just to me?* She held her breath, instantly searching for any noise or threat. Had Gabriel found her?

A soft tap sounded on the door.

"No!" Piper screamed inside her head. She stood up quietly with Stanley held tight to her body. Grabbing her phone, she snuck to the door. Piper held her breath as she leaned forward to peer out the peephole. Air gushed from her lungs.

"Easton!" Piper called as she fumbled with the lock and door handle. Rushing into the hall, she stepped into his arms and laid her head on his shoulder.

"Shh, Little girl. I didn't mean to scare you. It's okay. Daddy's here," he said softly, rubbing his hands along her spine and holding her close.

Piper pressed against him, feeling her heart rate slow as she absorbed his warmth. She inhaled and breathed in the masculine scent that was purely Easton. After several seconds, she leaned back self-consciously.

"Sorry. I'm so glad to see you. Aren't you supposed to be at your dinner meeting?" she asked.

"Never be sorry to see your Daddy." Easton pulled her back to him and pressed a kiss on the top of her head as he squeezed her close.

Then, taking one step back, he smiled at her before taking her hand and leading her through the apartment door. With his free hand, Easton closed and locked the door. "Come sit down," he urged as he tugged her gently to the plush sofa, where he guided her onto his lap.

"I could sit next to you," she whispered, holding Stanley close.

"You could, but I've waited all this time to get to you. I need to have you close. Who's this?" he asked, running a finger over the teddy bear's fur.

"Stanley," she squeaked. "He's my best friend."

"Hi, Stanley. I'm very glad to meet you. I'm glad you're here with Piper."

"Why are you here?" she asked, peeking up at him.

"I didn't want to be anywhere else. I hoped you might come stay with me tonight."

"I don't sleep around," she said defensively.

"Good. I don't sleep around either. I've been looking for my Little girl for a very long time. Two years ago, I decided I wouldn't have sex with anyone I couldn't see as mine forever. I knew that either I'd find you or you'd run into me. I wanted to be free for us to build our lives together."

"Our lives together," she echoed.

"Yes, Piper. I'm a firm believer that in life we have one soulmate. I thought I'd found my one twice, but we both knew quickly it wasn't right."

"You think I'm the one?"

"I do. Can you see me as your Daddy?" he probed.

"Yes. But I'm scared."

"I know. If I could go back in time and scoop you up before the fake Daddy lured you in, I'd pay… well, I'd cash in Edgewater Industries and all I own," he confessed, tucking a strand of hair behind her ear.

"You haven't known me for long."

"How long did you have Stanley before you loved him?" Easton asked.

"About two minutes," Piper admitted.

"I've had you in my life a bit more than two minutes, and I plan to keep you close just as you hold on to Stanley. Will you let me show you how a real Daddy cares for his Little girl?"

Daringly, she pressed her lips to Easton's. She needed to make sure she hadn't imagined the connection she'd felt earlier with the handsome man. Easton's mouth moved gently under hers, teasing her lips apart. Responding instantly to his silent request, Piper threaded her fingers through his thick hair and wiggled closer.

"Mmm! Little one, you taste so sweet," Easton complimented before stealing more kisses.

Distracting her completely from any worries, he explored her body with a lingering touch, as if he hated to leave one sweet curve to sample another. Easton eased her back on the soft cushions of the sofa to hover over her protectively. Piper basked in his attention, feeling more beautiful than ever before.

When he lifted his hand to span her ribcage, Piper inhaled sharply. "Please," she whispered, unable to control her plea.

"Are you ready to be mine, Little girl?" he asked, brushing back the hair from her face and kissing down the sensitive cord of her neck as he granted her wish.

He cupped her breast, brushing his thumb over her sensitive nipple. The jolt of his touch arced straight to her pelvis. Piper lifted her lower body to his warmth and froze at the feel of that thick erection pressing into the soft skin of her stomach. By instinct, she brushed her pelvis against his cock, feeling the wetness building between her legs. She wanted him.

A sharp pinch of her tight peak shocked her into meeting his gaze.

The heat reflected in those gorgeous green eyes mesmerized her. She needed him.

"Answer the question, Little girl." His voice was pure velvet over steel.

Struggling to remember the question he'd asked her, Piper looked at him in total confusion.

"Are you ready to be mine?"

Her head nodded without waiting for her brain to decide. The words spilled from her lips. "Please, Easton!"

Without asking another word, Easton rose from the sofa and quickly scooped her up in his arms. He carried her to her rumpled bedroom and placed Piper gently on the bed. Stepping back, he cupped his erection and stroked from the base to the tip before he slowly unbuckled his belt.

Piper watched him pull the leather band from his slacks. A fantasy flashed into her mind as she imagined Easton using this implement to correct her behavior. When he placed the belt on the bed next to her, she stared at it for long seconds as the image of her lying over the bed with her legs dangling over the mattress edge as he spanked her thoroughly with it ran through her thoughts.

"Have you been bad, Piper?" His deep voice invaded her imagination.

Looking up at him in shock, she shook her head rapidly. "No, Daddy. I've been very good. I promise."

Easton leaned over to slide a hand under her head and raised her lips to his for a hard kiss. His fingers tangled in her hair and tugged, giving her a flash of pain that increased the heat between her thighs. "Daddy knows Little girls need guidance to behave properly."

His hand stroked down her side to glide between her body and the soft bedspread. "I will not hesitate to spank this bottom with my hand, belt, or perhaps another implement?" he suggested.

When her gaze darted from his face back to that leather band next to her, Piper whispered, "I'll try to be good, Daddy."

"That's my girl," he praised her as she rose to standing once again.

Instantly, she missed his heat. Piper pushed herself up on her elbows as his fingers deftly unbuttoned his crisp dress shirt. She started to sit up, but settled back into place when Easton shook his head at her. "I'd like to help," she protested.

"You do not have permission, Little girl."

The answer was definite. Easton's voice held a strength and power that she couldn't resist. He was in charge.

She concentrated on the vee of tanned skin that widened with the release of each fastener. Piper knew what was hiding underneath the professional attire. When the urge to touch him became too much, she curled her fingers into the soft material below her. As he pulled the tails of the shirt from his waistband and shrugged out of the fabric, she devoured his torso from afar.

"Good girl," he praised, pulling her attention from his chest.

"I'm trying to follow your directions."

"Thank you, Piper. Well-behaved Littles earn rewards," he shared with a knowing smile. Easton flicked the button of his slacks open and glided the zipper down.

Staring at the thick head that surged through, Piper unknowingly licked her lips in anticipation. His answering groan halfway through her unconscious action drew her attention to the movement. Looking up at him, she held his gaze as she finished deliberately. Piper loved the desire reflected in his eyes that revealed she could affect him as well.

When Easton pushed the slacks over his hips, she ripped her attention from his face to watch the material slide down his thighs to puddle at his feet. Unable to resist, she traced his fierce erection with her gaze. Piper held her breath when he hooked his fingers into the waistband of his snug boxer briefs to lift them over the head of his shaft. Her concentration intensified as he pushed his underwear over his hips and down his legs.

Mesmerized by the total picture Easton provided as he stood proudly, allowing her gaze to travel over his body, Piper felt spellbound. A sound of protest fell from her lips when he moved, disturbing her view.

"Soon, Little girl," he promised as he stepped out of his shoes and pants. Leaning over, Easton stripped off his socks. He kicked his clothes to the side to approach the bed. After tucking a small packet under the edge of the pillow, he brushed his fingers through her hair.

"Now it's your turn, Little girl." Easton scooped Piper into his arms and gently set her feet down on the floor. He smoothed his hands over her outer thighs, capturing the hem of her nightshirt and raising it slowly over her hips.

His gaze held hers. Piper shivered as the oversized garment rose. His hands caressed her ribcage, freezing the air in her lungs. Easton stepped closer, pressing his lower body against hers. The air gushed back into her lungs at the feel of his cock brushing against her intimately as he tugged the shirt slowly upward.

"Raise your arms, Piper."

As she followed his directions, he whisked the garment over her head and let it drop to the floor. Easton ran his hands down her arms to foil her automatic instinct to cover her body. "Let me look at you, Piper. I want to see my beautiful baby."

Piper stood straight, thrilled by the hunger etched on his face. His hand lifted from her forearm to draw a line from her lips over her throat. He pressed a warm kiss to the sensitive spot where her neck and shoulder merged. Rising, Easton's focus shifted lower as he trailed his fingertips over the swell of her breast and circled her nipple, watching it tighten even more.

"Daddy, please!" she whispered.

"I need to taste your sweetness," he answered before taking that budded tip into his mouth to roll it between his lips. He supported her with one hand wrapped around her side when she swayed toward him.

The heat of his mouth surrounded her as he sucked her nipple into his mouth. His tongue lashed across the tender tip, making her knees weak. Piper clung to his shoulders as her lower body arched toward him. She loved the feel of his cock pressing into the soft swell of her tummy.

"Make love to me, Daddy," she pleaded when he lifted his head from her breast.

"That's what I'm doing, Little girl. I don't plan to rush." He turned and led her the short distance to the bed. Throwing the covers open,

Easton crawled onto the bed as she tried to memorize the display of his muscular buttocks.

Easton moved the pillows to settle against the headboard. He patted his thighs before holding his hands out to invite her to join him. "Come on, big eyes. Come sit on Daddy's lap."

When she followed his movement, Easton guided her to sit astride him. Taking her mouth in a hungry kiss, he stroked down the outside of her thighs before trailing his fingertips lightly up the inside of her legs. Automatically, Piper tried to pull her knees together, but his body blocked her movement. She watched as Easton raised his fingers, coated in slick wetness.

"You are so responsive, Little girl," he praised her. "I think you need a reward, don't you?"

Piper nodded quickly, eager to see what his reward would be. She squealed as his thighs below her shifted apart, widening hers as well. Easton stroked her intimately. Taking his time, he explored her pink folds slowly as he searched for those special pleasure spots. Once he found one, he experimented with different types of touches until she writhed on his lap.

Mindless as the sensations overwhelmed her, Piper closed her eyes as she caressed his lightly furred chest and traced the muscles in his torso and arms. When Easton pressed one finger deep into her core, Piper cried out as her body clamped around the invader. Pure pleasure exploded inside her as Easton continued to stroke the arousing points he'd discovered.

He gradually lightened his touch, allowing the bliss to dissipate. Finally able to think, she blinked her eyes open to stare into his. He looked at her with an expression she'd never seen before. Sexual hunger mixed with enchantment as if he were delighted by her response. Her climax had brought him pleasure as well.

Leaning forward, Piper pressed her mouth to his. Her tongue wrestled with his as she tempted him to make love to her fully. To her delight, Easton wrapped his arms tightly around her and rolled their bodies, trapping her below him.

"I need to be inside you, Piper," he whispered against her lips.

Piper nodded eagerly and slid her hand under the pillow to

retrieve the condom he'd placed there earlier. "Can I help?"

"You can touch Daddy later, Little girl," he answered with a shake of his head, rising to his knees above her.

Disappointed, Piper concentrated on his promise to give her permission later and stared openly at his body displayed before her. Her hands caressed his strong thighs as he ripped open the small packet. Her breath caught in her throat as he stroked his hand from his balls to the tip of his cock. The erotic sight of him touching himself fueled the already burning heat in her core.

Sheathed by the thin protective layer, Easton spread her thighs and placed the head of his thick shaft at her entrance. Slowly, he forged his way inside her, ensuring Piper's body had time to stretch. When she tried to buck up toward him to hasten the process, Easton anchored her against the bed with a firm hand pressed against the curve of her stomach. Being restrained boosted her excitement.

He's in control.

When his pelvis met hers, Easton leaned over her to press hard kisses to her lips. "You feel so good, Piper."

Pleased by the compliment, she wiggled below him, drawing a groan from both their lips. Easton shifted backward, withdrawing from her heat, and thrust back inside to brush against that hidden button at the top of her channel. His initial slow motions sped up as she wrapped her legs around his waist to pull herself to him as he entered.

Their bodies blended into a natural rhythm. Straining together, sweat gathered on their skin, making them slide against each other. Piper inhaled deeply. She loved Easton's hot, aroused, masculine scent. On an impulse, she tasted the skin of his throat by running her tongue up the cord of his neck. When he bucked forward a bit deeper, she knew she'd found one of his sensitive spots. Piper bit down lightly on his skin and wiggled happily at the low groan that emerged from his throat.

"You're playing with fire, Little girl," he growled softly into her ear.

Her response? Scattered nips and kisses on his skin as she explored how to bring him more pleasure. His hand slid under her bottom to tilt her pelvis slightly as he stroked inside. Piper gasped as tingles gathered between her thighs. His thrusts now pressed directly on her clit. When he circled his hips to grind against her body, she exploded around him.

"Ahhh!" escaped from her mouth as her hips chased his touch. To her delight, Easton paused while pressed deep inside her as he repeated that circular motion several times. When it became too much, she unconsciously dug her fingernails into his broad shoulders. Easton readjusted to short strokes in and out of her tight passage.

When she'd recovered slightly, Piper stroked over his chest and pressed kisses to his salty skin. "More, please," she whispered. "Come with me."

His mouth captured hers in a deep kiss before he answered, "Together this time."

Stroking deeply into her body, Easton built the pace. Heat gathered around them as their bodies strained together. Everything faded into the background as their world narrowed around them. As Easton loomed over her, Piper caressed him, loving the feel of his corded muscles beneath her fingertips.

She could feel her climax approaching as those delicious tingles gathered between her legs. Piper stroked her hands to his buttocks as she fit herself against his pelvis. "Now, Daddy. Now!"

"Together, Little girl," he commanded, quickening his pace even faster.

With a cry, Piper came hard, clamping around his thick cock. She loved his answering groan as he thrust deep inside her body. Feeling him throb within her, a brief wish flashed through her mind to feel his skin against hers completely. *Soon*. Piper abandoned herself to the cascade of emotions and sensations that flooded her.

Later, as she lay cuddled against his chest, Piper crossed her fingers, hoping with the last of her energy that this amazing man would stay in her life.

"Shh, Little girl. Enough thinking for the day. Sleep now," his low voice commanded.

Without protest, she snuggled closer and closed her eyes. Tumbling into sleep wrapped in his arms, Piper enjoyed the sweet dreams that came from pleasure and safety.

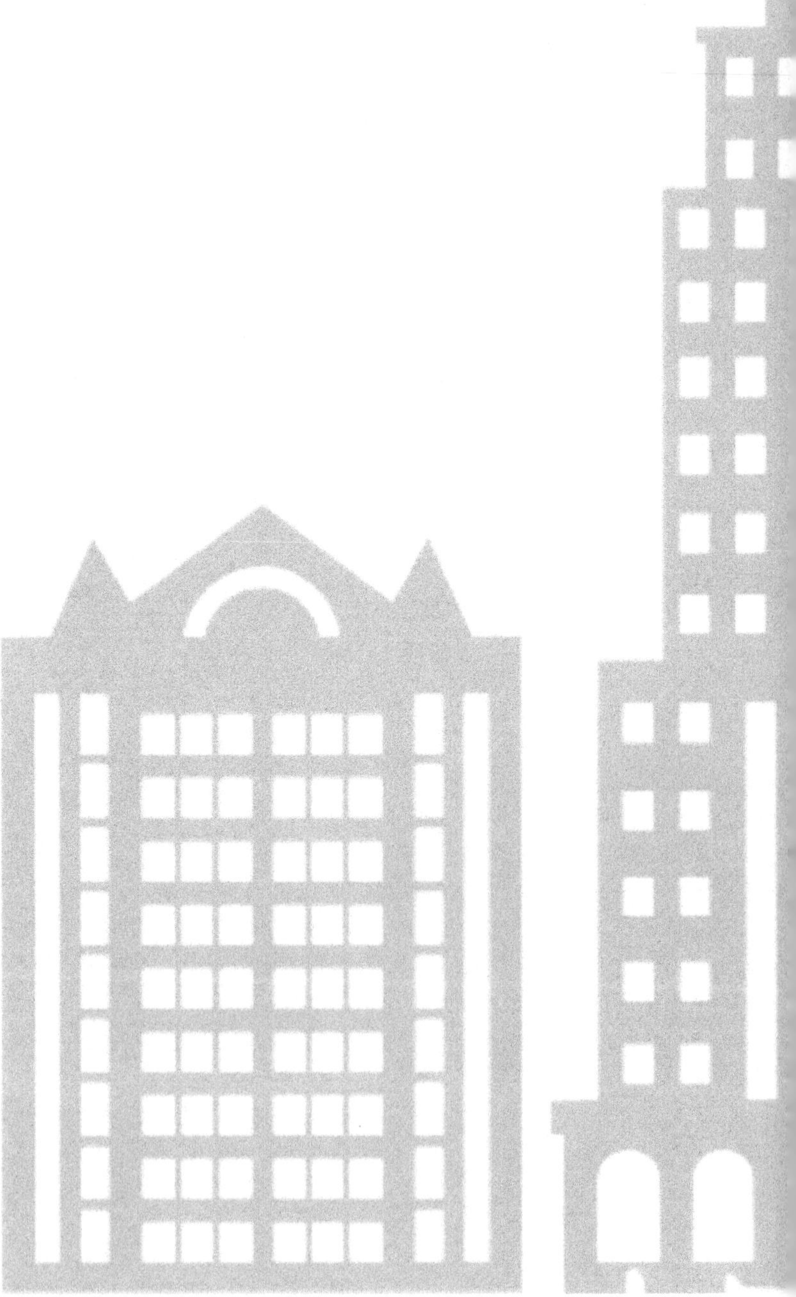

CHAPTER 11

With his good morning kiss lingering on her lips, Piper applied her makeup. She'd slept better than she had since leaving Gabriel. Easton's presence protected her from all those lingering nightmares and bad thoughts. Piper smiled at her reflection. Who was she kidding? Easton made everything amazing.

He'd left that morning after holding her close to whisper his happiness in finding her. "You pleased me last night, Little girl."

His praise echoed in her mind after he left to change clothes. She set down her mascara with a click to stare at herself in the mirror. *What happens if he decides he doesn't want me anymore?*

In her veins, Piper's blood seemed to turn ice cold. A workplace romance could have terrible results. Having an affair with the president of the company could be the stupidest move in the history of blunders. Was she making a huge mistake?

Piper turned to walk into the bedroom. Easton had made up her bed when she'd run to the restroom. Standing at the foot of the bed, she noticed he'd tucked her sweet stuffie into the covers with his head resting on one pillow. She wrapped her arms around herself.

Shaking the negative thoughts from her mind, Piper vowed to judge Easton only by his own actions. *He's nothing like Gabriel.* Feeling herself smile once again, Piper stepped into her closet to choose her clothing carefully for the day. She wanted to look especially good for the man who meant so much to her already.

In just a few minutes, she dashed out of her apartment. Catching the elevator just as it started to close, Piper squeezed through the doors and greeted the woman inside. "Hi, Regina, right?" she double-checked that she remembered her name correctly.

"Yes! And you're Piper. Good morning. You look rosy and refreshed this morning."

Trying to keep herself from blushing furiously, Piper changed the subject. "I haven't run into you since that first day. You must be really sticking to taking the stairs."

"Most days I'm really good. Today, I woke up with the blahs."

"Yuck. I've done that before—almost every Monday!" Piper laughed.

"I'm glad I'm not the only one."

Waving goodbye to Regina as they parted to head to their respective offices, Piper hoped she'd cheered up the other woman a bit. She wanted everyone to feel as good as she did. Eager to see Easton again, Piper walked quickly across the garden area to A tower.

When the elevator doors opened into her office, Piper stepped out with a smile, ready to call a good morning to Easton. The rumble of voices in Easton's office silenced her greeting. Piper stowed her purse and sat down to start her computer. As it powered on, she made two cups of coffee, adding a heavy stream of honey into one, and carried them into Easton's office.

"Good morning, gentlemen," she chirped when they noticed her entrance.

"Thank you, Piper," Knox said with a smile. "And thank you for the coffee." He accepted the cup and took a large sip, groaning with delight at the caffeinated brew.

"Piper," Easton greeted her with a warm smile. He took the coffee from her hand and wrapped his arm around her waist to pull her closer to his chair. "We're talking about Gabriel Serrano. I want you to know what's happening." He placed the cup on his desk and drew her onto his lap.

Automatically, she tried to scramble away. *Surely I shouldn't sit on his lap in the office... with a witness!*

"Stay here, Little girl. I need to hold you close," he corrected, tightening his arms around her.

"But..." Piper looked meaningfully at Knox.

"Knox knows you're my Little. It's okay."

"Really?" Piper looked at Knox in astonishment. "How do you know?"

"Daddies recognize a Little when they are lucky enough to meet one, Piper. I promise not to reveal your secret to anyone. You can decide who needs to know. As the head of security, I protect all the precious Littles who work or live in the ABC Towers."

"You... You're a Daddy?" she asked hesitantly.

"I am."

"Do you have a Little girl?"

"I know who my Little is. She's not ready for my care yet," he shared.

"But she will be in the future?" Piper asked. When the words left her mouth, she waved a hand between them. "I shouldn't have asked."

"Her life is in turmoil now. I'll be there to pick up the pieces."

Piper nodded. Easton had helped her immensely in such a short time. She wanted that for Knox's Little girl as well.

"What's going on?" she asked, leaning forward to snag Easton's coffee. She took a large drink before handing it to him.

Chuckling at her drink thievery, Easton hugged her closer. "Knox's men stopped a visitor early this morning. His ID listed him as Gabriel Serrano. He requested to see you."

"He knows where I am? Can he get in?" she asked quickly as she huddled next to Easton's strength.

"The guards did not admit him onto the grounds. They instructed him to leave and with a few choice words, he complied," Knox said evenly.

"Am I safe here? Do I need to look for another job somewhere else?" Piper asked.

"You're not going anywhere. I have my lawyers working on a restraining order to keep him away," Easton assured her.

"He's never going to follow that." Piper's mind whirled with all the things she'd seen Gabriel do. Once he had his mind made up, he never changed it.

"You are safe here. Look at Knox. Do you think he's going to let a con man get through the gate?" Easton gestured to the large man glowering on the other side of the desk.

"N-no," she admitted hesitantly.

"You can make that a definite no," Knox suggested.

"He's sneaky," she warned.

"No," Knox repeated.

"You can't stop everyone," Piper pointed out.

"Watch me."

Silence filled the room as the men waited for her to process through Knox's promise. After several long seconds, Easton raised his coffee cup to his lips and took a drink. After lifting it to toast Knox, he offered it to Piper. Still lost in thought, Piper accepted it automatically and sipped the hot brew.

"Okay," she said finally.

"Knox thinks he's tracking your phone. Would you let him take your cell for a few hours to have an expert look it over?" Easton requested.

"Of course." Piper wiggled to get to her feet and dashed from the room to dig her phone from her purse. After handing it to Knox, she settled back on Easton's lap abstractedly.

"Thank you, Piper. Easton, I'll be in touch." Knox rose to his feet and left the office.

Easton set his coffee cup back on his desk and turned his full attention to Piper. "Now, Little girl, give me a quick kiss before my meeting starts in two minutes."

She glanced behind her to see the screens lighting up, showing that someone waited to be connected to the meeting. "Oops. Sorry." She pressed her lips to Easton's. As she lifted away, his hand glided through her hair to cup the back of her head. Holding her in place, he kissed her thoroughly. When he released her, they were both out of breath.

"Go, Little girl," he directed, pulling a handkerchief from his pocket to wipe her lipstick from his mouth.

"Here," she said, taking the soft cloth from him to wipe the last vestige of pink from one corner of his mouth.

With a cheerful wave, she darted from the room. Seconds later, she heard Easton greet everyone and apologize for the brief delay. She glanced at the clock to see he'd started the meeting slightly after the normal time. Piper felt her lips curve into a delighted grin. Easton thought kissing her was more important than the movers and shakers he talked to every day.

The morning flew by. As one meeting ended, another started. When she'd come back from her lunch break, Piper discovered Easton's door was closed. She set the sandwich she'd brought for him to eat in the refrigerator that always held bottles of cold water. Nabbing one for herself, Piper returned to her desk and fumbled in her purse for her bottle of over-the-counter pain tablets.

She dropped two in her mouth and washed them down with the cool liquid. Pressing a hand to her stomach, Piper cursed the onset of her period. She'd have to buy tampons tomorrow. Picturing the aisles at the company pharmacy, Piper figured they'd have those in a pinch. Remembering the city she'd driven through on her way to the ABC Towers, Piper knew she'd seen a retail store on her path. She filed that away for when she needed a variety of supplies.

The medicine dulled most of the pain, but by the end of the day, Piper was ready to curl up with a heating pad on her stomach. With a groan, she remembered she hadn't thought to bring that with her. She'd have to buy one. The warmth on her abdomen made the cramps so much better.

"Knox asked me to bring this to you," Pete's gentle voice reported, pulling her attention back to the office.

"Thank you!" Piper took the cell phone with a smile. She was so used to having it with her, it felt weird when she didn't.

"No problem. He said the expert had found nothing in it. He turned off the tracking that had been enabled on the phone."

Piper shook her head, regretting her habit of sleeping soundly. What else had Gabriel done while she was unconscious? She waved as Pete turned to leave. "Thanks again!"

Looking at the closed door, Piper decided to text Easton with the message she needed to run to the store. Quickly, she typed in a message. *Going to the pharmacy for some supplies.*

Almost immediately, he answered. *Don't go off-grounds. Remember, there's a pharmacy in the C building. Go there.*

She sent him back a red heart emoji and turned off her laptop. Grabbing her purse, Piper walked past building B to the last towering office building. Waving her badge at the attendant at the desk, she walked to the elevators. A directory on the wall provided the floor for the pharmacy. She pushed the two and waited.

Sharon had explained that access to some floors required clearance from the desk. Others, like the cafeteria or, in this case, the pharmacy, were available at all times to everyone. Thankful she didn't have to share her reason for visiting the store, Piper rode the car up one floor and followed the signs.

"Can I help you?" a friendly voice asked.

Piper turned around to see Tess. "Hi! I'm glad to see you again."

"Hi, Piper. I haven't run into you since that first night."

"Unpacking is no fun," Piper laughed.

"Ugh! I still have some boxes," Tess commiserated. "What are you looking for?"

"I need some tampons and a heating pad."

Tess shook her head. "The last heating pad we had in stock just walked out the door. More are coming tomorrow. I'll hold one for you if you'd like."

"I'll just come back tomorrow for it," Piper answered quickly. She didn't want to take advantage of their friendship.

"Okay. Let me show you where the feminine products are." Tess led her to the correct aisle. When Piper had the boxes she needed, Tess plucked a paper sack from the top shelf and put them inside. "You're all set unless you need some pain relievers?"

"I've got those. What do I owe you?" Piper asked, looking around for a cash register.

"Everything is free here, Piper. Mr. Edgewater provides health supplies for his employees. This is an amazing place to work. Come back tomorrow and pick up a heating pad."

"Thank you, Tess."

Walking out without paying felt weird. She sent a mental thank you to Easton for creating such a supportive company. Piper had never heard of anyone who provided everything for their employees.

A twinge in her stomach made her hesitate as she passed the parking lot. Heat on her stomach would help so much. The store wasn't far. She could get there and be back in twenty minutes. Impulsively, she found her car and backed out of the parking spot. Waving at the security guard at the gate, Piper missed his concerned look when the sensor beeped as it scanned her ID. The gate rose, and she drove through.

Two minutes later, her phone buzzed. "Easton?" Piper said, looking at the name displayed on the screen.

"Where are you going, Little girl? It's not safe to be off the grounds." His low voice held concern in every syllable.

"I just need to run an errand."

"Come back and we'll send someone out for you."

After Gabriel, Piper had promised herself that she'd never allow someone to have total control of her—to make decisions she didn't want to follow. She hesitated for a minute and then turned off the phone. No one was going to tell her what to do. *Not even Easton.*

Concentrating to remember where she'd passed the store, Piper missed the black sedan that pulled out of a parking lot behind her. She celebrated when she spotted the familiar logo ahead. Within a couple of minutes, she skipped through the door and headed toward health care to look for a heating pad.

As she passed the candy department, Piper suddenly craved chocolate. She turned down one aisle and then backtracked to the previous one to find the brand she loved. A scent caught her attention and she looked around. Piper would never forget Gabriel's favorite cologne. It was linked in her mind with him.

Peeking out around the shelving, she didn't see any sign of her former lover. A man with a small child in a shopping cart was a few steps away. *Maybe he wears the same cologne?*

Abandoning the idea of chocolate, Piper scanned the other shoppers as she walked toward her targeted department. Finding the right section of the store, she searched through the display and couldn't find the heating pads. There was a jumble of items on the bottom shelf. Piper squatted down to double-check and grabbed a box triumphantly.

"The last one!" she announced to the empty space around her.

"To the victor go the spoils," quoted a very familiar voice as a pair of highly polished shoes appeared in Piper's line of vision.

Bolting upright with the box held before her as a shield, Piper met Gabriel's dark eyes. They'd always reflected his emotions: passion, anger, excitement, and approval. Now she read triumph in his gaze.

"Gabriel, I wasn't expecting to see you here."

"I'm sure," he answered with an evil smile as he moved closer. The familiar scent of his cologne underlined his presence, sending an icy shiver up her spine.

"What do you want? I returned your ring." Piper tried to present a strong, confident appearance even as her heart beat faster.

"You have been very bad, Little girl. Your punishment will be severe this time."

Piper swallowed hard and saw the triumph again in his eyes. *Don't show weakness!* She pulled her shoulders back and shook her head, trying to look confident. "You don't have any right to punish me, Gabriel. You're not my Daddy."

"I'll always be your Daddy, Piper. That gives me every power to correct you. Let's go. Set the box down and we'll leave so we can hold this discussion privately." He nodded at an older lady who eavesdropped as she pretended to scan the painkillers nearby.

"I'm not going anywhere with you, Gabriel. Our relationship is over. Besides, I no longer work at my old job. You can't use me to benefit your company."

"But now you work for Edgewater Industries. I'll be pleased to have an ally in that company," he said, stepping forward to reach for her arm.

Piper danced backward to avoid his touch. "Leave me alone, Gabriel. If I have to, I'll get a restraining order."

"That will do you no good. You are my fiancée. No judge will award such a barrier between lovers."

"I'm going to get the manager. You need to leave that woman alone," the older lady said from the end of the aisle. She pushed her cart quickly toward the front of the store.

"Old biddy!" Gabriel scoffed before pacing forward. "Time to leave, Piper."

"Uff!" The air gushed from her lungs as she quickly backed away, ramming into a large, immoveable object. Immediately, she tried to scramble away, but an arm wrapped around her, holding her in place. Craning her neck to see who held her, Piper blinked when a bright flash of light blinded her momentarily. The inability to see skyrocketed her panic. She struck at the man holding her.

"Piper, it's Knox. I've got you," his deep voice reassured her.

"Knox?" she questioned. His hand patted her waist reassuringly. Piper blinked to restore her vision and noticed Knox's hard glare never wavered from the other man.

"Piper does not wish to go anywhere with you, Gabriel Ernesto Serrano. She has told you this. I am a witness, as is the older lady at the front desk who has asked the management to call the police. I believe they are on the way. The security cameras will be a great aid in a court case." Knox pointed up to the bubble over their head on the ceiling that silently recorded the encounter.

To confirm his statement, an announcement sounded in the store. "Security to aisle twenty-seven, please. Code blue."

"Knox! Thank goodness you're here," Piper thanked him. She scurried behind him to peek around his bulk at her ex-Daddy. "I will never have anything to do with you, Gabriel. I think you've shut down your chances at doing business with Edgewater Industries as well."

Knox nodded to confirm her suggestion, making Gabriel's dark expression look even more angry. "There's no way to win here,

Serrano. Cut your losses and leave. If not, Mr. Edgewater will ensure that no one does business with you again."

"Indeed I will," Easton guaranteed from behind Gabriel.

Instantly, a mask dropped over Gabriel's face as he turned a charming smile on Easton. "Mr. Edgewater, I am glad to meet you," he said, holding his hand out to shake Easton's.

Piper attempted to run to him, but Knox held his arm out to block her movement, softly instructing, "Let your Daddy handle this. Watch."

When Easton didn't respond to his gesture, Gabriel dropped his hand awkwardly and continued, "You know how Little girls are. They like to be bratty from time to time. Piper will change her story soon."

"What?" Piper sputtered in indignation. "You… You…"

"Your time with her has ended. She will never return to your care. I pity the Little girl who ends up with a man who has no clue how to be a Daddy," Easton scathingly stated.

Sirens sounded from outside. A man behind Easton announced, "There was a report of a disturbance in this aisle. I'm going to ask all of you to step outside to speak to the police. Anyone who does not cooperate will be subject to arrest."

"But nothing has happened here," Gabriel assured the security man.

"Please exit the store, sir."

Easton stepped out of the aisle and held a hand out, indicating that Gabriel precede him. With a snort of disgust and anger distorting his face, Gabriel stalked from the aisle toward the front of the store. Piper flew around Knox to throw herself in Easton's arms, crushing the heating pad box between their bodies.

"Little girl, you are in so much trouble," he whispered against her hair as he held her as close as possible. "What did you need so much that you risked your life?"

Sheepishly, Piper stepped back to display the damaged container. "It was stupid, but I thought I could zip in here and I'd feel better."

The eavesdropping security man looked at the smashed box and rolled his eyes. Piper felt her face heat even more. "It was important."

"No one should keep you from getting what you need," Easton

commented softly. "You could have asked someone to get it for you or to accompany you, Piper."

"Sir, I'll ask the three of you to go to the front of the store, please."

"Of course. Come, Piper. We'll get this settled."

As they approached the front entrance, they passed the service desk. A woman behind the counter watched in fascination at the unfolding events. Easton took the crushed box from Piper and set it on the counter with money to cover the cost.

"Could you ring this up for us while we're outside?" he asked pleasantly.

The bewildered employee looked at the security guard for guidance on what to do.

"Process the sale. If he's taken away by the police, he'll forfeit the purchase," he instructed.

"Thank you, sir," Easton said pleasantly.

As he steered Piper outside, a duo of officers separated them to get their stories. Piper was tickled to see that Gabriel talked to another, and so did the older woman who'd helped her inside. She explained to the officer what had happened several times. Soon, he asked her to stay in one place as he conferred with the officers who'd talked to Easton and the older woman. Glancing at Gabriel, who now glowered at her threateningly, Piper wanted to stick her tongue out at him, but refrained—barely.

Her stomach pain worsened as the painkillers she'd taken wore off. Piper pressed a hand to her abdomen and just wished to go home. *This was the worst decision ever! Who am I kidding? Dating Gabriel topped that by a mile!*

Peeking over at Easton, she found him watching her. His forehead wrinkled with what she interpreted as concern. "I'm okay," she mouthed to him. A movement caught her eye and she watched one of the police officers handcuff Gabriel.

"What? You can't arrest me! My lawyer will have me out of there before the ink dries," Gabriel threatened.

"We let the lawyers do their jobs and we take care of ours," the patrolman answered evenly. "Get in the squad car, please."

Gabriel continued to sputter. His voice died away with the firm closure of the rear door, sealing him inside.

"Ma'am? It's pretty clear that you are the victim here. Thank goodness for your protectors. There are a lot of women who aren't so lucky. We're going to take Mr. Serrano in on harassment charges. Since he didn't touch you, that is the most serious charge we can process. He'll be out quickly. Make sure you're safe when he's released," the uniformed man suggested. His eyes revealed a world of experience.

"Thank you, sir. I think those guys are going to keep me safe," Piper assured him, nodding at Easton and Knox.

"Stay alert."

She nodded and watched him walk away. Easton wrapped an arm around her and pulled her close to his side. He turned her away from the sight of Gabriel yelling from inside the squad car.

"It's time to go home, Little girl. Let's get your heating pad and head back to the ABC Towers," he suggested. When she nodded, Easton left her with Knox to step in to pick up her bag.

"I'm sorry, Knox."

"I know, Little girl."

"How did you know I needed help?"

"The security desk notified me when you left. They should have kept you from leaving until I reached the gate. There will be some additional training immediately," he said, glowering.

"I followed you when your call with Easton ended abruptly and he couldn't reestablish contact." Knox looked at her before raising one eyebrow.

"I was stupid."

"Your safety was more important than the meetings Easton had on his schedule. I happened to be close to my car, so I followed. Your ID tag has a short-range locator. As soon as you stopped and I got close, I could pinpoint your location."

"And Easton came, too."

"We talked as he caught up. I let him know where you'd gone."

Easton returned with his purchase. "Ready to go home?" he asked.

"Please."

CHAPTER 12

Easton helped her change into comfortable clothes and settled Piper and her stuffie on the couch in her apartment with the heating pad on her stomach. "Take these," he directed, holding out two painkillers and a glass of milk.

"I'm sorry."

"I know." Easton settled next to her on the couch and wrapped an arm around her shoulders. Instantly, she cuddled next to his chest.

Sure that his feelings would have changed about her, Piper studied her stuffie's brown fur. Her parents had always teased her about her fascination with the stuffie. She'd received it as a present for her second birthday from her grandmother. Everyone had suggested alternatives they liked better than her choice. No one seemed to understand that Stanley was her new best friend's name, not Piper's invention.

"Was Stanley worried about you?" he asked softly.

"Yes," she admitted. "He never liked Gabriel, but I didn't listen to him. I thought he was just jealous."

"What does he feel about me?"

Piper lifted her furry friend to her ear and listened to his response. She kissed his cheek before settling him back on her lap. "Stanley tells me I need to apologize a hundred times and hope you'll forgive me.

He says only someone who cared about me a lot would have followed me and tangled with Gabriel."

"That's true. Stanley is a very discerning bear. I'm glad he gave you a positive report about me."

"I'm sorry," she repeated. *That is five times at least.*

"You don't need to apologize a hundred times. I have a feeling if you could go back and change how you handled that, you would do things completely different."

She nodded vigorously and withdrew from Easton to slouch back against the couch in misery. Piper felt awful. She'd screwed up everything. On top of the stupid decision she'd made, her stomach hurt, and her emotions were raw. Tears coursed down her face.

Could life get any harder?

"Little girl, you're making my heart ache." Easton lifted her onto his lap and held her close as he rocked her gently from side to side.

"Do you want me to leave?" she wailed. Her tears became a storm of unhappiness at the thought of leaving him. She had to ask. It was better to rip the bandage off all at once.

"No."

His brief answer startled her. Blinking away the moisture from her eyes, she leaned back to study his face. "That's it? No?"

"I don't want you to leave. You're my Little girl. I need you with me."

"I don't want to leave…" Her voice trailed away as she digested his words. "You still want me for your Little girl?"

"My heart has made its decision. You are my Little girl."

"Even if I really mess up?"

"Even if you completely do the absolute wrong thing, you're mine."

"Are you going to spank me?" she fretted.

"I don't think you're ready for me to spank you. One day, you'll have enough trust in me that you'll allow me to correct your behavior. Littles always feel better when their poor choices are wiped away by punishment."

"I trust you," she rushed to tell him.

"I want you to trust me here," he said, laying a hand over her heart, "as well as here." Easton brushed his fingers through her hair and pressed a kiss to her forehead.

Unable to lie to him, Piper nodded. She knew he was right. "I'm sorry."

"No more I'm sorries. He misled you and treated you poorly. You were brave and daring. You reached for your dreams and fantasies but were deceived by a con man. Now you know what qualities you need in a Daddy."

Piper met his gaze. "I know exactly who my Daddy is."

Easton leaned forward to kiss her hard. "That makes me very happy, Little girl." He held her close once again and rocked her gently.

This time, her emotional stress and her physical symptoms combined to make her sleepy. She felt so protected in his arms. Within minutes, she escaped into sleep, cuddled on his hard chest as he took care of her.

She awoke in her bed with Stanley cuddled to her chest. The heating pad placed carefully over her tummy had helped keep the cramps at bay. Needing to care for herself, Piper rolled out of bed and froze at the sight of Easton's bare back emerging from the covers. Her fingers tangled in the hem of her oversized nightshirt she didn't remember putting on last night.

He slept here?

Easton had obviously gotten her ready for bed and stayed with her. Feeling her lips curve in a private smile, Piper walked to the bathroom. After caring for herself, she found the two painkillers Easton had left for her on the counter with a glass of water. Quickly, she took those and returned to crawl into bed.

"Okay, baby girl?" His voice reached out, rough with sleep.

"Better," she replied as she slipped under the covers.

Fitting her back against his body, Easton spooned Piper. His warmth felt so good on her lower back. She curled her knees up to ease her cramps. Did he know that menstrual pain was worse if you stretched out straight?

"Thank goodness for life experiences," she thought, closing her eyes as he pressed a soft kiss to her hair.

He was there for her. Even when she had no desire for physical shenanigans and just wanted to survive the discomfort of her monthly cycle, Easton wanted to take care of her and make her feel better. She realized he wasn't a Daddy for the power or the fantasy. Easton would cherish her in all ways. Piper kissed the strong bicep wrapped around her shoulder.

"Sleep, Little girl," he directed.

Her mind quieted, and Piper tumbled back into sleep.

Easton carried most of her things from her apartment to his the next afternoon while she curled up on his leather couch. Now her clothes hung across from his suits and dress shirts. When everything was arranged as she wished, he'd ushered her back to the couch. Pulling a soft throw from the back of the couch, Easton had tucked it around her. He pressed a soft kiss to her lips.

"I'm glad you're here, Little girl. Let me get you something to drink."

"You don't have to wait on me," she'd protested as she'd curled into a ball.

"Let me get your heating pad first. Want some medicine?" he'd asked.

"No. I'll be fine with the heating pad. I'm sorry. I don't mean to be a bother."

Sitting down next to her, Easton tipped her chin up to meet his eyes. "You don't feel well, and I wish to care for you. That's what Daddies do."

When tears filled her eyes, he pulled her close. "The past is over. You're here now with me. Concentrate on us."

"Okay, Daddy." She straightened and wiped the tears from her eyes with her fingertips. Meeting his gaze, Piper whispered, "How did I get so lucky to find you?"

"I feel exactly the same way."

When she threw herself against him, Easton wrapped his arms

around her to hold her close. Aware that she didn't feel well, he shifted back after several long seconds. "Let's get you feeling better."

When she nodded, Easton kissed her forehead and retrieved her heating pad. After placing it on her tummy, he filled a tumbler with ice water and snapped the lid and straw in place so she wouldn't have to worry about spilling. He even opened up his stash of flavored popcorn so she could have a snack.

After he showed her how to use the remote, she quickly found an animated movie she'd never gotten to watch. Cuddled on the couch, Piper sighed contentedly. "Thank you."

"I have just enough time to go for a run before dinner is ready. Are you okay if I leave you alone?"

"Yes." She blew a kiss at him before turning back to the characters on the screen. Popping a few kernels into her mouth, Piper seemed to forget he was even there.

With a laugh, Easton jogged to the master bedroom to change into his running clothes. When he came back with his shirt slung over his shoulder, Piper paused the show to study him with hungry eyes. "I'll be back soon. Explore if you get tired of the show. There's only one locked door. I'll show you that room this evening if you'd like."

"What kind of room?" she asked. Her voice wavered slightly, revealing her nervousness.

"The nursery," he answered, and saw her eyes light up. It would do her good to wonder about that room.

"I'll be back soon!" he promised.

Running down the steps, Easton started his workout. He smiled as he estimated how long it would take her to explore the apartment. Easton loved Piper's curious mind. The questions that she asked at work made him stop and reconsider how he and Sharon had always done things. Often, she had insightful suggestions.

Now he knew that inquisitiveness would propel her off the couch to look in all the nooks and crannies. Easton didn't want her to feel awkward about looking around. She already felt guilty about so many things. Soon, she would be ready to ask him if she could turn over all her worries to him. Accepting punishment for the mistakes that had blossomed into vast craters in her mind would allow her to dismiss those bad feelings once and for all. Little girls shouldn't fret about things in the past. Especially when she had not earned the blame.

Damn Gabriel!

He'd check with Knox to see what his contacts in the local police force could report. Hopefully, Gabriel would cut his losses and move on. If not, he would discover that Easton would protect his Little girl with all his influence and power. Piper would not be subjected to the manipulative man again.

"Hi!" Piper clicked off the TV as Easton walked into the apartment.

Bare chested and gleaming with sweat, he looked like he should be on the front page of Silver Fox magazine—if that even existed. She stood and walked toward him, allowing her gaze to feast on the handsome display.

"Don't get too close, Piper," he warned, holding a hand up to ward her off.

"I don't mind a little perspiration," she shared, drawing a finger down the center of his glistening chest. Feeling daring, she leaned forward to kiss him before licking a path down his neck to his collarbone. His deep moan kindled a distinct warmth in her abdomen. It was so much better than her precious heating pad.

"Would you like me to make love to you, Little girl?" he asked, pulling her flush against his body.

"I'm on my..." Her voice faded away with embarrassment.

"Daddies don't mind if their Littles are messy. I want you to be comfortable as well as turned on when I make love to you."

Piper ran her hand down his arm to link her fingers with his. He understood everything. How did she get so lucky? "Thank you," she whispered.

Easton lifted their clasped hands to press a kiss on her fingers. "I always want you to tell me how you feel, okay?"

When she nodded, he added, "How about if I shower and then we explore together?"

"I'd like to see the nursery."

"Your nursery, Little girl," he clarified before pressing a kiss to her lips this time before turning to walk into the master bedroom.

As she watched him walk away, his toned ass almost changed her mind. Almost.

CHAPTER 13

With tousled wet hair and comfortable clothes on, Easton appeared in the doorway. Her fingers itched to comb through his salt-and-pepper hair, making her smile at her reaction to his devastatingly casual appearance. *I have it bad!*

He jingled a set of keys and asked, "Ready to explore?"

"Yes," Piper cheered, jumping to her feet.

"This room will stay unlocked from now on. I closed it when I despaired of ever finding you. Now that you're here with me, it's ready to welcome you."

Quickly, he inserted the key and clicked it open. Twisting the knob, he pushed the door open. Unable to curb her curiosity, Piper stepped forward. The room seemed to draw her inside. She looked around in amazement.

"It's beautiful!" she said in awe, walking forward to place a hand on the pale pink wall with raised panels. The beautiful paint sparked with flecks of color. "Is this glitter?"

"Unicorn blend," he confirmed.

"These are the prettiest walls ever!" she exclaimed, tracing the grooves in the decorative panels. Turning slightly, she looked at the beautiful bed. "Am I going to sleep in here?"

"I'd prefer you sleep with Daddy, but Little girls need a space of their own sometimes. This would be a good place to nap," he suggested.

Piper walked forward and ran her hand over the silky comforter. It was so soft and inviting. "Stanley would love this."

"Stanley is welcome to play in here. There are some more toys in the big chest," Easton pointed out.

"I see it." Piper didn't want to leave the bed. It was so pretty. Gauzy white fabric draped from the ceiling to loop around the four posters that rose from the corners. She climbed up on the bed and looked around.

"It's not dusty in here," she observed.

"No. The cleaning lady makes sure that it's always ready."

"Has anyone slept in this bed?" she probed.

"Only me. Lie back on the pillows."

Nestled against the mound of softness at the head of the bed, Piper wrapped her arms around herself. "I love this."

Easton crawled onto the mattress and lay on his side next to her. "I'm glad. If there's something you don't like, we can change it."

"No!" jumped from her throat.

When he looked surprised, she added, "It's beautiful and I feel so safe here—like this is the place I can just be me."

Easton brushed his fingers through her hair and leaned in to kiss her lips. "This is your haven, Little girl. It's your place to be happy and loved. It's also a safe spot to experiment and see what you need most while you're Little."

"Experiment?" she repeated.

"Yes. Try different things to see if you like them. Like…" Easton rolled over to open the bedside table. He pulled out a small pink container and opened it to reveal something sealed in plastic. Dropping the container to the bed to free his hands, he tore the packet open. "Try this."

Piper opened her mouth automatically when he brushed the nipple across her lips. Experimenting, she sucked lightly on it. It felt… Quickly, she pulled it from her mouth when she noticed him watching her.

"I'm not a baby," she refuted.

"You're a beautiful woman. I hope you know I want you to explore all your dreams and desires. Your paci is a small part of trying new things. Sometimes, it will be perfect from the beginning. Other times, you'll need to experiment several times. You never have to be worried about what I'll think. Remember, I bought it in case my Little would enjoy it."

Easton drew her hand back to her mouth. "Try it again," he suggested.

When she popped it into her mouth, he showed her what else was in the packet. "Look, Piper. You can decorate it the way you want. There's a space on the front to put these little beads and you can even add your name or other words if you like."

Piper took the packet of fun decorations and scanned the contents. She plucked the paci from her mouth and looked at the front. "They all go here," she observed. "That's fun. I could even change it from time to time."

"You could switch it up as often as you wish," Easton assured her. "I think you'll nap deeper with your paci, but we won't know until you try, right?" He held up the small container. "We'll store it here when you don't want it."

She carefully placed it inside when he opened it. To her surprise, she felt disappointed when he snapped the top into place.

"Ready to go look at the toy chest? I think you'll find some fun things in there, too."

Leaving the pretty bed reluctantly, Piper allowed her curiosity to make her move. She knelt in front of the chest and reached out to lift the top. "Wow! Look at all the coloring books, and I love colored pencils. I haven't played a board game for years. And puzzles! We could put these together after work," she suggested, unconsciously rubbing her stomach.

"I'd love that. We can spread out all the pieces on the table. We have a little time before bedtime, but I think you need to finish your movie. Shall we wait to play with your new toys?"

Nodding, Piper tucked several items back in the toy chest. She hesitated for a few seconds before scooting over to him and wrapping her arms around Easton's waist. "I'm so glad you found me. Thank you for all these fun things that you're sharing with me."

Easton kissed her tenderly. His hand soothed over her and rubbed at the small of her back. "I've dreamed of you for so long. I'm glad I've found you, too."

After holding her for several minutes, he gave her one last squeeze. "Come on, Little girl. I can hear your heating pad calling your name."

Playfully, he pitched his voice toward the door, pretending to be it. "Piper…"

"Daddy!" she laughed and let him help her off the floor.

CHAPTER 14

The next few days went smoothly. Piper felt so much better physically as her period lessened and ended. Each day, she fell a bit more in love with her handsome Daddy with every moment she spent with him. Sleeping and waking up in his arms each morning started her day off perfectly.

Her Daddy seemed to have totally forgiven her. Easton didn't bring up her mistake to leave the grounds without telling anyone. Piper appreciated it, but felt it lingering in her mind when she had quiet minutes to think about her actions. How could she have been so stupid?

Pulling her attention back to the phone, she realized that the other woman had gone quiet and waited for her to say something. Quickly, she came up with something that would fill the gap. "Thank you for all your help, Sharon. I think I'm figuring it all out. I'll call next week if I have questions," Piper said. She disconnected the call after they'd both said their goodbyes.

Get it together, Piper.

A sound at the door drew her attention away from herself. Piper smiled as Easton's second in command strode purposefully into the room. Elaine Rivers exuded power and control. Her leadership style was diametrically opposite Easton's. Piper had discovered since she arrived that the combination of the two meshed perfectly. The employees gravitated to one or the other's communication style. If Piper were honest, the administrative assistant in her appreciated Elaine's checklist of requests that showed up in her email.

Today, Elaine walked in shaking her head in disbelief. "Can I swap you for my assistant?"

"No." The definitive answer came from Easton's doorway. "Fane is perfectly suited for you."

"He bought me a kite and says we're flying it tonight after work. He's in there right now putting the thing together."

"How many times have you double-checked the report for the board tomorrow?" Easton asked quietly.

Elaine looked at him in surprise. "I've definitely made sure that you'll have the correct information," she rushed to assure him.

"The first version was sufficient."

"This is an important decision," Elaine pointed out.

"It is. The information you compiled was intrinsic to my decision. Come in and let's make some plans."

Easton looked at Piper and requested, "Don't allow anyone to interrupt us, please."

"Yes, sir."

His answering wink at her answer made her face heat as her heart skipped a beat. The submissive response wasn't quite right, but she couldn't call him Daddy in the office, right?

Piper opened a new document on her computer and got to work creating the template that Easton had detailed for her in the preparation notes for the meeting. Halfway through, she stopped to proofread her work and gasped when she saw the word punishment listed not just once, but three times. She dropped her head down on the wooden desk and bounced it a few times.

She was going to have to deal with it. The guilt she felt about doing the wrong thing wasn't leaving her mind. Obviously, it was getting worse when the thoughts were ricocheting in her brain.

An hour later, Elaine left Easton's office with a wave and a resigned, "Guess I'll go fly a kite."

"Have fun!" Piper wished her, glancing at the clock to see it was past time to leave for the day. She didn't feel sorry for Elaine. Only someone completely out of touch wouldn't have seen the excitement on the usually stoic woman's face. Easton's second in command might complain about her after work plans, but she was looking forward to them. Besides, Piper liked Fane and thought he was perfect for the work-driven woman.

As soon as Elaine left the office, Piper stood and walked to Easton's desk. He looked up from a stack of papers and said, "Just a few more minutes and we'll close up the office for the night."

"I want you to punish me," Piper blurted, and immediately felt her face heat with embarrassment.

"What am I punishing you for, Little girl?" Easton asked gently as he rose from his chair to circle the large polished desk, getting close to her.

"I didn't follow your directions, and I left, putting myself in danger," she admitted.

"This is weighing on your mind?" he probed.

"I hate that I screwed up being your Little girl already."

"Daddies don't keep a record of good deeds and poor choices, Piper. You never need to worry that I'll stop caring about you because you made a mistake."

"But I know I hate that I did something so stupid. I can't forgive myself," she confessed, feeling the tears tumble from her eyes to roll down her cheeks.

"Come sit on my lap, Piper. I need to hold you," Easton commanded, wrapping an arm around her waist to guide her to his chair. The moment he sat down she scrambled onto his lap.

"Daddy!" Piper wailed as she buried her head against his chest. She felt absolutely miserable.

Easton rocked her in his arms until her sobs quieted. When she peeked up at his face to judge his reaction, he dropped a light kiss to her forehead. "I think it's time you felt better. Go lock the office door and come back here."

He helped Piper to her feet. At his doorway, she paused to look back at him. Easton nodded to encourage her. "Go lock the door."

Piper heard his movements as she left the office and knew that he was clearing his desk for the evening. He wouldn't spank her in his office, would he? She'd never be able to work there without remembering. Quickly, she flipped the lock on the desk and powered off her computer as well. Finally, she looked back into his office.

"Come on in, Little girl. We'll go to your nursery." He held out a hand for hers.

"You're not going to spank me here?" she asked.

"No. I'm not going to spank you there, either. I think you've had enough of that punishment for a while," Easton commented as he drew her through the adjoining door into his apartment.

"You're never going to spank me?" she asked.

"Yes. You'll lie over my lap bare-bottomed in the future. Just not this first time," he explained.

Piper had told him about getting spanked by Gabriel when she'd woken up from a nightmare about him. Finding Easton's arms around her had helped dispel her panic. It had also been easier to confess while encompassed in a shroud of darkness.

"Clothes off for punishments," Easton announced as he turned her around to unfasten the back of her slim skirt. It tumbled to the floor before she processed that she would be naked.

Standing perfectly still, Piper felt her panties drop to the carpet as well. Half-exposed seemed more naked than being nude—at least until he drew her shirt over her head and unfastened her bra. Easton helped her step out of the pile of clothes around her. She fixed her gaze on the floor. Piper watched his polished leather shoes move as he moved to stand in front of her.

Easton drew a line down the outside of her arm from her shoulder to her clasped hands. She shivered in reaction to the light touch. When he wrapped one large hand around her wrists, she jumped slightly and tugged away. Caught securely in his grasp, Piper squeezed her thighs together, feeling herself becoming wet. What would he choose for her punishment?

"I've considered a variety of consequences for your behavior, Piper. Writing sentences, standing in the corner, going to bed without eating dinner; all seem too light in consideration of the risk you took.

Giving you an enema could help clear the darkness you're holding inside."

He laughed when she looked up at him for the first time with a shocked expression. "I see you hadn't considered how intimately I will care for you, Little girl."

Easton paused, letting that thought rumble around in her mind. "That, however, is not what I have chosen." He reached up to press a decoration on the paneled wall. A large section slid to the side revealing a selection of implements.

As she gasped at the display, he explained, "I will paddle you in the future, but for now, we'll use this." He selected a coiled length of cord. Deftly, he wrapped the silken rope around her wrists.

After tying it, he instructed, "Try to pull your hands free, Little girl. I want you to realize that you are fully restrained so you won't fight it."

Piper tried to free herself and failed. Holding her hands out to him, she lifted her head to meet his gaze. "I can't."

"No," he confirmed.

"What are you going to do to me?" she asked.

"I'm going to punish you." Easton's deep voice held a tone of caring that she had gotten used to while staying with him.

Piper's emerging panic from being restrained eased at his matter-of-fact tone. She nodded. This was what she needed. "Will I feel better?"

"Later, Little girl. You will feel much better. Come." He pulled her over to the center of the implement display. "Turn sideways," he directed before lifting her hands over her head to loop the binding over a deep hook. Easton adjusted it upward until she stood on the balls of her feet.

"Perfect. You are exquisite," he praised, scanning her body before cupping one breast and rubbing his thumb lightly across the beaded tip.

"No!" she protested as he lifted his hand.

"It is not time for pleasure, Little girl, but for the punishment you need."

A click behind her alerted Piper that he had selected something.

Unable to turn around to see it, she could only wait. Her breath caught in her throat.

"Tell me what you are about to be punished for, Piper."

"What?" She tried to turn to look at him, but Easton stabilized her position easily.

"Why have you asked me to punish you?"

Having to announce it out loud to the empty room made it worse. She swallowed hard before allowing the pent-up words to tumble from her lips. "I knew Gabriel could be out there. I knew he had threatened me. But despite the risk I knew was out there, I didn't ask for help and I hung up on you when you called to check on me. I tried to do everything myself."

"Thank you, Little girl," Easton said as he stepped back into her view. He held something that looked like a metal spatula.

"This is an electric paddle. It is a simple implement to use. There is very little impact. I will simply touch you with it lightly." Demonstrating, he drew a line diagonally across her stomach.

"It just feels cool," she whispered in confusion. *How is this punishment?*

"You must trust your Daddy." Easton flipped a switch on the bottom of the device and Piper heard a low buzz and felt an electric wave brush against her.

"You stated five things that you needed to be reprimanded for. Four will earn you five touches each. The final one will earn you two minutes."

Before she could do the math in her head, Easton drew the edge of the implement across her outer hip. She gasped as a thin line of electricity crackled across her skin. The fine blue trace bordered the line between pain and annoyance. The longer it rested on her body, the more difficult it was to stand still. The static charge made the fine hair on her skin stand up, adding to the sensation. Piper tried to convince herself that it didn't hurt—much.

"That is what you will feel. On your hip, it's disturbing but not damaging. On other places, the feeling will change." Easton touched the tip of her breast.

"Ah!" Piper cried, curving into herself as the zing went through her sensitive nipple. Instant arousal filled her body. She closed her eyes, trying to hide her reaction from him.

Continuing, Easton applied the device all over her body. The snap and crackle made the device sound dangerous. She dreaded the tingling charge she knew she'd feel next. A caress of his hand followed frequently to soothe her but couldn't ease her trepidation. She never knew what his target would be. Twisting from the hook, Piper abandoned thinking. Able to concentrate only on her punishment and the growing need inside her, Piper waited for the next zing and sizzle.

"Twenty," his voice announced, sounding husky to her straining ears. She heard a soft thud before his hands roamed over her body, checking to make sure she was okay.

When he was before her, Piper arched her body to press herself against him as much as her restrained wrists would allow. "Daddy!" she cried, needing him.

"I'm here, Little girl. I'll always be here." Her Daddy's arms encircled her body, holding her tight.

Panting, Piper listened to his steady heartbeat as his warmth eased into her naked skin. She could feel the soft scratch of his fine wool suit jacket against her skin. His scent grounded her. This was her Daddy.

"Is it over?" she whispered when she could talk.

"Two minutes more. Are you ready?" Easton tilted her chin up to see her face. He studied her expression before kissing her lightly. Reaching above her, he lowered the hook a few clicks, letting her ease down to rest fully on her feet.

"Spread your legs, Piper."

She shifted her thighs apart, obediently following his directions. Her breath caught in her throat as he stroked down her side and trailed his fingers across her abdomen. When his fingers slid between her legs, she rose back to her toes. *He knows!*

"My Little girl needs a reward for being brave during her punishment."

She seized upon his words. This time, she didn't feel dirty after her punishment had aroused her. Her bravery had earned a reward for being brave.

Easton slowly caressed her intimately. Sliding his fingers through her drenched pink folds, he sought the spots he knew brought her pleasure. Piper could feel the slickness of her juices coating the tops of her thighs, revealing her reaction to her punishment.

"Daddy. I've been so good."

"You have. Let's finish this so I can hold you."

She heard another click as he pulled something from the display. Feeling something cold brush against her thigh, Piper looked down her body to see a large wand vibrator with a rounded head. As she watched, he placed it between her legs and adjusted it to fit intimately against her inner lips. A tug on the hook above lifted her back to her toes, drawing her thighs together to trap the device in place.

Click.

Buzzing filled her thoughts as her body reacted instantly to the stimulation. Piper twisted, pulling the cording that bound her as pleasure coursed through her body without pause. Climaxing over and over as the vibrator delivered her final punishment, she heard his low voice announcing the time in thirty-second intervals.

"Two minutes."

"Daddy!"

"Ninety seconds."

"No more. I'm sorry."

"Sixty seconds."

"I'll be good!"

"Thirty seconds."

"I can't."

"You can do anything, Little girl."

Finally, the buzzing stopped. She sagged, unable to hold herself up, shuddering as he removed the wand. When he wrapped one arm around her to hold her tight, she felt his hand lift hers from the hook. Boneless, she collapsed against him as he praised her softly. The words didn't matter. She couldn't concentrate enough to understand.

The need to be close to him filled her as he lifted her in his arms to carry her to the soft bed. Piper pressed herself to her Daddy as he stretched out next to her. The feel of the comforter wrapping around her made her exhale with happiness. He was here with her. Her Daddy had wiped away everything else.

CHAPTER 15

Piper woke sprawled over Easton's body. He held her wrapped in his arms on the chaise lounge on the balcony. Her loving Daddy had moved them outside when she hadn't been able to stop shivering. The early evening sun still radiated heat.

Unable to resist the opportunity, Piper studied his face as he looked over the railing. The experience lines faded into faint traces on his relaxed features. She found she missed them. The laugh lines at the corners of his eyes and mouth witnessed how often he smiled. Concentration lines between his eyebrows proved his dedication to work. His features attested to all that was good.

An image of Gabriel's handsome face popped into her mind. It seemed blurry and out of focus. She had trouble remembering insignificant details like whether he had freckles scattered on his nose or if his mouth tilted up or down at the corners while he slept.

Dismissing him from her thoughts, Piper focused on the handsome man below her. His breath soft and regular, she moved slightly to trace his vision and laughed at the huge octopus kite with its tentacles flowing in all directions in the clearing in front of the towers.

"You're awake. How do you feel?" he asked, looking concerned.

She traced his whiskery cheeks and chin with her gaze to give herself time to decide how to answer. Overwhelmed with the desire to feel that stubble rub against her skin, Piper shifted to brush the side of her face against his.

She turned to meet his gaze and answered, "I feel good. Amazing, in fact." Leaning forward, she kissed him deeply.

Green eyes reflected his desire as she pulled back to look at him. Without a word, Easton cupped the back of her head and pulled her down to his lips once again. Tasting her deeply, he explored the inside of her mouth as he took control of the kiss. His lips and tongue teased and tantalized as he devoured her.

Suddenly, nothing was more important than feeling him against her skin. Piper unbuttoned his shirt by feel as she funneled all her desire and feelings into her kisses. Pulling the tails of his dress shirt from his waistband, she spread her fingers over his chest and threaded them through the silky hair over his torso.

With the last of her willpower, she pushed away from his body. "Easton?" she whispered. "Are you sure I'm your Little girl?"

"I know you are mine, Piper. I'm just waiting for you to decide if you belong with me."

Piper opened her mouth and Easton placed two fingers over her lips to stop her from replying automatically. "You're close to being able to make that decision. I won't accept less than all of you. Until you're ready for that level of commitment, I'll be here. There's no timetable for love." He slid his hand to tangle through her hair, falling forward to create a curtain of intimacy around them.

"You love me?"

"I love you, my Little girl. When you're ready, you'll share your feelings with me. For now, I need to feed you. Something fast and easy. Scrambled eggs for dinner?"

Her stomach growled loudly between them, bringing a low chuckle she loved from her Daddy's throat.

"Breakfast for dinner it is!" he announced.

P iper tried to curb her happiness as the board members filed out one by one with pleased smiles. Easton Edgewater was Edgewater Industries. He had created the board to be a type of second eyes to review the decisions he made and offer differing views if they had questions.

She'd taken notes throughout the meeting as Easton and Elaine worked smoothly together to update everyone on the progress of the company. Their preparations had been spot-on. The reports had thoroughly detailed the last six months of business. Hearing their profile of the company, Piper was extremely proud of the intelligent and resourceful man she'd fallen in love with.

That thought rocked her as she automatically looked to Easton for reassurance. His eyes met hers. Immediately, he headed toward her. Piper held up a hand with a smile to signal to him she was okay. The handsome business owner nodded slightly and turned back to the assembled group as they milled around the large office space.

When the elevator doors finally closed to carry the last group downstairs, Easton wrapped his arms around her. Lifting her feet from the floor, he twirled her around in a circle. "They loved you. The older ones don't like change. I knew they'd miss Sharon, but everyone sang your praises. Good job, Little girl. We need to go celebrate. Grab your purse."

As they headed for his car, Easton's phone rang. "Hello?" He paused. "Hold on a minute. I want you to repeat that but let me put you on speaker. I'm here with Piper." He turned the speaker feature on and held the phone between them.

"Go ahead, Knox."

"Hi, Piper. Congrats on the success today. Everyone was raving as they left the building."

"Thanks, Knox!"

"I called to tell you both that the private detective who's been checking in on Gabriel reported today that he's returned to Argentina. He took with him a young woman from one of Easton's competitors."

"Oh, no! She doesn't have a clue what he's really like." Piper instantly felt for Gabriel's newest victim.

"She'll figure it out. Her family is very wealthy. He may play it cool for a while to stay in contact with her money," Knox suggested.

"However it goes, it sounds like they'll have money to come to her rescue if needed," Easton reassured her.

After a brief conversation, Easton disconnected and guided Piper to the sedan. "Don't worry about her, Piper. They say everyone has a match. Perhaps she's his."

Deliberately pushing it out of her mind, Piper leaned forward to kiss him. "I hope everyone finds their perfect companion. Choose something that's fast to eat, Daddy."

"Why?"

"You're going to want to bring me home early," she said with a smile as he helped her into her seat and secured the belt over her lap.

"Really?"

She nodded and watched him walk around to the driver's side. Piper could read the speculation on his face as he watched her through the windshield. She waited until he started the car and turned to look over his shoulder to back out.

Leaning close, she whispered, "I love you, Daddy."

The car stopped. Easton looked at her for several seconds before hauling her to him. His lips devoured hers as he hugged her as close as possible. A blaring car horn made him look up.

"Come on, boss. I want to get home to my sweetie, too. And congratulations to you both!" a familiar voice called through his open car window.

"Thank you, Jason!" Easton answered with a wave.

"Little girl," he warned, setting her safely back into her seat. Concentrating, Easton guided the car from the parking spot and out of the lot.

"Spaghetti. We can eat pasta fast." He held out his hand for hers. "I love you, too, Little girl. Let's go celebrate."

ELAINE

Elaine pushed her glasses up to rest on the top of her head as she forced herself to look away from the computer screen. This status report took several days to complete each quarter. The challenge of pulling together myriad different bits of information into a consolidated document stressed her out completely.

An air horn bleated incredibly close. Jumping from her seat, Elaine stood next to her desk, attempting to control her racing heartbeat for several seconds before dashing into the adjourning room. A handsome young man looked up from her assistant's desk with a grin.

"Sorry. I bet that interrupted your train of thought. I'll put it in the bottom drawer," he apologized.

"Who are you?"

"I'm Fane—your new assistant. Sharon picked me out of the admin pool to come replace your old one. You go through a lot," he shared as he pushed up the black-rimmed glasses that did nothing to disguise his good looks.

She stared at him, unable to answer that. Good assistants were hard to find. Elaine would hold on to one as soon as she found the right fit. It wasn't her fault that she expected the highest level of competence and dedication.

This man would have been her absolute last choice. Laughter lines bracketed his mouth and his brown eyes twinkled. With finger-tousled hair and cuffs rolled up to reveal elaborately tattooed forearms, there was no way he fit the professional profile she needed to greet visitors to her office.

Trying to pull her eyes away from the charismatic man, she noticed the large box sitting on the desktop. A variety of brightly colored items spilled over the top: a Frisbee, a large tie-dye colored stuffed bear, a plastic golf club, a wooden handle… that wasn't a… Elaine looked at him in disbelief.

"I don't think this will work, Fane…" Elaine began, trying to be diplomatic.

"Sharon told me not to let you scare me off. She thought you needed something different." He spread his arms, drawing her attention to his toned body. "You got me."

Closing her mouth with a snap, Elaine pivoted and stalked forward into her office, slamming the door behind her. *We'll just see about that!*

Thank you for reading Daddy's Waiting! Find out what happens next in Elaine's story in Daddies Watching.

What happens when she reaches the top of the ladder and finds herself alone?

Elaine Rivers works hard, but having fun is much more difficult. As the powerhouse of the Edgewater Company, there's no shortage of pressure in her life. In fact, if it weren't for her new goofy administrative assistant driving her crazy, she might never experience any fun.

Fane Bogart has loved Laney for a long time. When a chance to step directly into her life appears, he jumps on it to be close to her. Finished with watching from afar, he knows all her secrets and is ready to take control. Can he use his playful charms to earn her trust and her submission outside of the office?

One-click Daddy's Watching now!

Don't miss future sweet and steamy Daddy stories by Pepper North? Subscribe to my newsletter!

I'm excited to offer you a glimpse into Daddy's Watching, book 2 in the ABC Towers series

One-click Daddy's Watching now!

5.0 out of 5 stars
Loved Daddy's Watching
Reviewed in the United States on February 2, 2022
Pepper North has done it again! She always gives me characters I absolutely fall in love with, they are so real that you could bet that you have passed them on the street or sat next to them in a diner. While Elaine is Easton's second in command at Edgewater Company, she is found to be really hard on any PA who is assigned to her. That is, until Fane comes into the picture. He is not only a top PA, he just happens to be a Daaddy who is intent on bringing some fun and discipline into Elaine's life before she gets burned out as a workaholic. Don't miss reading this book and all the fun, it is definitely worth the five-star rating.

5.0 out of 5 stars
Awesome book!!
Reviewed in the United States on April 3, 2020
I so totally loved this book!! A very special connection between a Daddy and his Little girl is amazing!! I fell totally in love with the characters and their story!! Lots of hot steamy sexy times adds plenty of spice to this book!!

5.0 out of 5 stars
Loved it
Reviewed in the United States on February 7, 2022
Absolutely loved this story! It's about a young woman discovering who she is and coming to terms with it. Elaine is the CEO at Edgewater Industries and just can't keep an admin. That is until Fane comes into her life. He knows that Elaine is his Little Girl, but needs

to show her that she is it for him. Elaine feels like she needs to prove herself and can't show her little side. So it's up to Fane to help her.

I am totally in love with Fane! He's kind, caring and totally hot! And Elaine has certainly met her match with him. She's a strong willed, career minded woman who needs someone to take care of her. Could that person be Fane? These two had such incredible chemistry and I loved their interactions. It's a delightful read and a great addition to this series!

Daddy's Watching - Chapter 1

"Let me know when you have those reports, Elaine," Easton Edgewater requested from the door to her office.

"Will do. I'll get them to you as soon as possible. I know there's a lot riding on how the numbers look this quarter," Elaine answered her boss as her fingers tightened on the folders in her hands.

"Take the time that you need for accuracy. I know these reports are a bear to complete, but you're right. Speed is important. I appreciate your efforts, Elaine. I couldn't ask for a better second-in-command."

Elaine nodded and turned into her office. It wasn't as elaborate as the CEO's, of course, but it was spacious and welcoming. She passed the empty desk with the cleared wooden surface with a grimace. *Damn, I need an assistant.* Once in her private space, she dropped the folders on the cluttered desktop and collapsed into her chair.

She gave herself exactly ninety seconds to whine inside at having to complete the reports. They were her least favorite thing to do. *I love seeing it all laid out for the company when it's finished.*

With that cheerier thought in mind, Elaine turned on her computer and got started. She was deep into the first set of data when an air horn bleated incredibly close.

Reacting instinctively, Elaine jumped from her chair. Standing next to her desk, she attempted to control her racing heartbeat for several seconds before dashing into the adjourning room. A handsome young man looked up from her assistant's desk with a grin.

"Sorry. I bet that interrupted your train of thought. I'll put it in the bottom drawer," he apologized.

"Who are you?" she asked, staring at the devastatingly charming man, filling the chair so attractively. With ruffled black hair and eyes so dark she could sense their color even from a distance, he presented such a picture that she had to school her expression into stern disapproval instead of drooling. That wouldn't do.

"I'm Fane—your new assistant. Sharon picked me out of the admin pool to come replace your old one. You go through a lot," he shared as he pushed up the black-rimmed glasses that did nothing to disguise his good looks.

That assessment stopped her from sightseeing. She stared at him, unable to answer his insinuation that she was tough to work with. Good assistants were hard to find. *I'll hold on to one as soon as I find the right fit. It's not my fault that I expect the highest level of competence and dedication.*

This man would have been her absolute last choice. Laughter lines bracketed his mouth and his brown eyes twinkled. With finger-tousled hair and cuffs rolled up to reveal elaborately tattooed forearms, there was no way he fit the professional profile she needed to greet visitors to her office, even in the black horn-rimmed glasses that partially cloaked his obvious wild side.

Trying to pull her eyes away from the charismatic man, she noticed the large box sitting on the desk. A variety of brightly colored items spilled over the top: a Frisbee, a large tie-dye colored stuffed bear, a plastic golf club, a wooden handle… that wasn't a… Elaine looked at him in disbelief.

"I don't think this will work, Fane…" Elaine began, trying to be diplomatic.

"Sharon told me not to let you scare me off. She thought you needed something different." He stood to spread his arms, drawing her attention to his toned body. "You got me."

Closing her mouth with a snap, Elaine pivoted and stalked forward into her office, slamming the door behind her. *We'll just see about that!*

She picked up the phone and called Sharon's cellphone. It

connected, and she heard the former executive assistant say as if she were a recording: "Welcome to Edgewater Industries, you've reached the Administrative Assistants Pool. We have restricted your privileges due to system overuse. Fane Bogart is your permanent assistant, with Easton Edgewater's approval. Have a good day."

"Sharon! Stop this nonsense. I can't work with this man... he brought *toys* to the office."

A click answered her statements as the phone disconnected.

"What?" Elaine looked at her phone in astonishment. Sharon had just hung up on her. "Enough!"

She'd handle this. Elaine walked into the outer office, ignoring her new assistant's cheerful welcome back as he decorated the top of his desk with a large blue stuffed bunny. Stomping out the door in determination, Elaine headed for Easton's office.

"I need to see Easton!" she barked on her way to the door. After attempting to twist the handle, Elaine turned to look at her boss's new secretary. "This is urgent."

"Mr. Edgewater left this note with me," Piper shared, lifting a small sticky note.

"Deal with it?" Elaine read incredulously.

"I know we don't know each other well yet, Elaine. I have gotten to know a lot of the other administrative assistants. He's the one everyone goes to when they need help with a problem. Everyone thinks the world of him. Give Fane a chance. There are several divisions that would leap at the chance to get him assigned for their group."

"They can have him. Fill me in on Easton's schedule. What's his first opening?"

Elaine watched Piper pull up a schedule on the computer. When Piper announced a date two months in advance, she stared at Piper in disbelief. "That can't be his first available appointment."

"Mr. Edgewater blocked out a freeze on changing employee assignments until that day. You can have the first time at eight," Piper offered cheerfully.

"This is ridiculous." Elaine turned on one high heel and returned to her office.

"How can I help you with the report?" Fane asked as she entered.

"Stay out of my office and be quiet," she hissed before closing the door. Elaine heard his response before it clicked.

"I'm here when you need me."

"Never!" Elaine swore under her breath.

Two hours later, she couldn't put it off any longer. Elaine had to use the bathroom. Standing, she paused to roll her head in a circle and wiggle her shoulders back into place. Tension from looking at all those numbers and stacks of data had given her a stress headache. Well, that and missing lunch.

She walked briskly to the door and paused with her hand on the knob. When she leaned in to press her ear to the wood, Elaine caught herself. No one would make her hide in her office! Flinging open the door, she strode through the outer office, rubbing her temple to try to ease the pain away.

"Good afternoon. I brought…"

Fane's words died out as she continued down the hall to the women's restroom. That would show him. She'd just ignore him.

Quickly using the restroom, Elaine washed her hands and wet a paper towel to wipe the back of her neck in a vain attempt to revitalize herself. She frowned at her reflection. Pale and drawn, Elaine looked just like she felt—overworked and stressed out.

Slower this time, she traveled through the hallway to her office. Pausing outside the door, she gathered her professional persona and walked into the office. Fane came out of her office with a smile.

"I just…"

"Don't go into my office. There is classified information on my desk," she snapped.

"I understand, Elaine. I didn't mess…"

"Good. Just leave me alone," she cut him off as she walked through the door and closed it firmly. Resting her forehead against the panel,

Elaine despaired. She'd never make it two months this angry at the incompetent man.

Turning to head to her desk, Elaine stopped in her tracks. Sitting on the desk was an iced coffee, a sandwich, two painkillers, and the stuffed blue bunny. She walked slowly forward to sink into her chair. Picking up the tablets first, she swallowed them with a sip of the drink. Elaine clapped her hand over her mouth to muffle the moan of delight at the delicious taste—exactly how she liked it.

Without thinking, she picked up the stuffie and hugged it. It was absolutely squishable and soft. Looking at the closed door, she felt bad. She wasn't giving him a chance. Fane had obviously gathered information about her favorite drink and had ordered lunch for her. In one half day, he had taken more interest in her than any of her previous administrative assistants.

At a light knock on her door, Elaine said softly, "Thank you."

"Need anything else?" he asked through the wooden barrier.

"No, this is great."

"Good."

She waited for him to say anything else, but Fane didn't. A few seconds later, she set the stuffie aside and picked up a sandwich half—turkey on wheat with mustard and sweet pickles. Her favorite. Taking a big bite, Elaine chewed in enjoyment. Within a few minutes, she tossed the wrapper in the trash. She'd been starving.

Elaine picked up her drink and took a long sip as she considered the door. If he kept the air horn and that embarrassing paddle put away, maybe she could deal with him. She decided to use the two months as a trial period. Pulling up her email, she sent Fane a message.

While I'm concentrating on these reports, I need you to set up two-hour meetings with the heads of each division beginning next month. Do not schedule more than one a day. The topic will be future expansion plans. They are to prepare a report of their current staffing and what they would need to handle a double workload. Thank you.

With that completed, she turned back to the report she was

compiling. After a couple of late nights, Elaine knew she'd be able to wrap it up. Losing herself in the data, she clicked through the next bit of needed information.

Want to read more? One-click Daddy's Watching now!

Dr. Richards' Littles®

A beloved age play series that features Littles who find their forever Daddies and Mommies. Dr. Richards guides and supports their efforts to keep their Littles happy and healthy.

Available on Amazon

Dr. Richards' Littles®
is a registered trademark of
With A Wink Publishing, LLC.
All rights reserved.

SANCTUM

Pepper North introduces you to an age play community that is isolated from the surrounding world. Here Littles can be Little, and Daddies can care for their Littles and keep them protected from the outside world.
Available on Amazon

Soldier Daddies

What private mission are these elite soldiers undertaking? They're all searching for their perfect Little girl.
Available on Amazon

The Keepers

This series from Pepper North is a twist on contemporary age play romances. Here are the stories of humans cared for by specially selected Keepers of an alien race. These are science fiction novels that age play readers will love!
Available on Amazon

The Magic of Twelve

The Magic of Twelve features the stories of twelve women transported on their 22nd birthday to a new life as the droblin (cherished Little one) of a Sorcerer of Bairn. These magic wielders have waited a long time to take complete care of their droblin's needs. They will protect their precious one to their last drop of magic from a growing menace. Each novel is a complete story.

Available on Amazon

Ever just gone for it? That's what *USA Today* Bestselling Author Pepper North did in 2017 when she posted a book for sale on Amazon without telling anyone. Thanks to her amazing fans, the support of the writing community, Mr. North, and a killer schedule, she has now written more than 80 books!

Enjoy contemporary, paranormal, dark, and erotic romances that are both sweet and steamy? Pepper will convert you into one of her loyal readers. What's coming in the future? A Daddypalooza!

Sign up for Pepper North's newsletter

Like Pepper North on Facebook

Join Pepper's Readers' Group for insider information and giveaways!

Follow Pepper everywhere!
Amazon Author Page
BookBub
FaceBook
GoodReads
Instagram
TikToc
Twitter
YouTube
Visit Pepper's website for a current checklist of books!

Printed in Great Britain
by Amazon